THE CURVEBALL

A Story of Grit,

Adversity, and

Winning the Game of Life

COLBY SHARMA

The Curveball

Cover design by Dane of Ebook launch

ISBN- 979-8-6895-1194-8

DEDICATION

To my dad, mom, sister, grandparents and family. Thank you for inspiring me to achieve my dreams and teaching me the invaluable lessons of persistence and daily practice. I couldn't have accomplished this without your love, encouragement, and support.

I felt driven to write this book because it encapsulates a lot of my personal experiences and the lessons I have gained. This book will show the power of putting ego to one side, the importance of mentorship when the going gets tough, and finally the power of believing in yourself no matter how challenging the circumstances.

FOREWORD

It's with great joy that I write these words, at the beginning of the first book written by my son.

We live in a time of deep chance and immense uncertainty. One can encounter this and retreat. Or you can embrace it—and grow.

The Curveball is a book for human beings who seek to turn fear into fuel, adversity into opportunity and hardship into hope.

...to face defeat and yet continue until you win is to walk the path of the hero.

...to know the pain of hurt and to keep chasing your dream is to soar with the angels, of your highest nature.

...to wonder if you're good enough to have the desires of your heart and still do the work required to make your vision real is to exemplify the magic that makes us most human.

You have your own unique form of greatness within you. You really do. No matter what your past has looked like and no matter where on the planet you live.

To neglect bringing your gifts to life is to deny us the benefit of your best.

So please read this book carefully. I've watched Colby working tirelessly on it, to ensure it brings special inspiration to you. Enjoy the story and then apply the subtle and beautiful wisdom you are about to learn.

Wonderful things will unfold for you. And you shining your light will soon make our world a better place.

Robin Sharma

Sometimes you have to lose
something, to find everything

CONTENTS

PROLOGUE
The Sound

It's a still, perfect day and Bryce Holloway is standing in a rectangle of white chalk on muddy earth.

The heat of the summer has settled like a blanket on what passes in Roarke County for a ball diamond. The outfield shimmers in the heat rising from the hardened ground. The stands, while full, are silent. It's too hot for noise.

Bryce wipes the sweat from his eyes, taps the plate with his bat one last time, and waits.

Bryce knows that ballplayers--the good ones, anyway--are *watchers*. You watch the pitcher for a tell. You check the outfield positions. If you're sneaky, you try to catch a glimpse of the catcher behind you shifting his position.

And of course, you watch the ball. Coach Teller had drilled that into his head over and over. Because good players *watch*.

But even at thirteen, Bryce wants to be more than good. He wants to be great. And so he's doing more than watch. He's *listening*.

The sound Bryce is aiming for is a sound like no other. A *thok* of leather meeting wood that, when it happens (which is never as often as one would like), means one thing: the ball is gone. Gone over the infield and gone over the fence.

For a boy of thirteen on a perfect summer day, that sound is everything.

And so Bryce stands at the plate doing just as Coach Teller

has taught him. He watches the pitcher, the fielders, the boys on base. He peers out from behind the locks of his sweaty blond hair, intensely focusing on the present moment.

But his ears are elsewhere. They are in the future, listening for the sound.

Alan, his nemesis, stood twenty yards away. On the Mount Everest of the diamond, the pitcher's mound, Alan's lip curls and in that moment, Bryce would swear he saw the boy sneering.

Then the sneer vanishes. The gloved hand hiding the ball from view rises to Alan's chest.

Bryce tightens his grip on the bat. Digs in his cleats. And the pitcher unleashes.

CHAPTER 1

THE LAST STRIKE

A *BANG* JERKS Bryce back to consciousness.

He flails briefly. His arms crash into metal and his legs jerk in spasm. His body is still in the dream, still in that hot, perfect, ball diamond, swinging for the home run.

His mind, however, is in the present and the present is a terrible place to be.

There are two reasons for this. The first is the headache. *Ow*, he thinks. That wasn't there yesterday.

The second is the shame. That, unfortunately, *was* there yesterday. And now it rises fresh, hotter than the ball diamond of his youth, moving through his now thirty-five-year-old body in a rush of blood.

Bryce is lying on the hard tile floor of the Darlington Dragons locker room with his head crooked painfully against a metal cabinet. His foot, which he can see without moving his head, has knocked a fist-sized dent in another locker down the line. That explains the bang, he thinks.

That same foot is wearing a cleat. And baseball socks. And as his eyes reluctantly move a little further, he realizes to his dismay that he's wearing his entire uniform. Shoes, cleats, jersey. The works.

That pretty much fills in the missing pieces of the story.

Good morning, sports fans, says the rich voice of a radio broadcaster in his head. It's early Monday morning and Bryce

Holloway, one-time first-round draft pick and now captain of the Darlington Dragons, is sleeping off yet another bender on the floor of the locker room where--

--a gentle cough cuts the mental voice short.

Bryce looks up from his awkward position to see the team's aging janitor looking anywhere but at Bryce. He stands, mop in bucket, gazing around the locker room like it's the most fascinating thing he's ever seen.

Bryce struggles to get semi-prone.

That's right, sports fans, semi-prone IS a lot like semi-pro!

"Hey, Willard," Bryce finally says.

"Hey, Mr. Holloway," Willard says.

Willard is now gazing intently at a flickering fluorescent tube in one of the overhead lights.

"Well," Willard finally says. "I guess Mr. Oscar wants to see you."

"Yes, I would imagine he does."

Bryce gets slowly to his feet. There's a large stain on his jersey. Right over the team logo. He doesn't want to know what it is.

He heads for the door, but then doubles back and heads for an open locker bay with the word "HOLLOWAY" stenciled to the top edge. He reaches slowly, his head pounding, into the top shelf and pulls out a tube of paper.

"Here you go," he says to Willard. "Theo, right?"

Willard takes the tube. He looks up at Bryce.

"Your grandson. His name's Theo? You said he was a fan. I signed it for him. There are tickets in there too--I thought maybe the family could come for my next..."

Bryce trails off. He looks at the dent in the locker. The stain on his jersey. "Anyway. There you go."

Bryce pulls himself straight, and walks smartly--at least that's what he hopes from the locker room.

There's nonsense. And then there's no-nonsense. And then

there's Mel Oscar.

As Bryce walks down the hall, he knows he's got a tongue-lashing coming. The GM of the Dragons isn't one for mincing words. He's the straightest of straight shooters and his temper is the stuff of legend. As Bryce rounds the corner to Mel's office, he braces himself for the storm, stopping just short of the open door to take a breath. Then he steps across the threshold.

Mel is sitting calmly at his desk.

Uh-oh, sports fans, the mental broadcaster says. *This is an unexpected surprise for hitter Bryce Holloway.*

It *is* an unexpected surprise. Mel Oscar stands as much as he shouts and until now, Bryce would have sworn the man's office didn't even have a chair.

"Morning, Bryce," Mel says softly. "Grab a seat." His pungent cohiba cigar fumes wafting through the air.

His voice is quiet. Even bordering on cheerful. And for the first time since becoming a pro ball player, Bryce feels a sensation he's almost forgotten: fear.

This isn't good.

And it isn't.

Bryce is in the meeting all of sixty seconds (no shouting, but the straight-shooting hasn't changed) and he finds himself back-pedaling. Retreating.

"Everyone has slumps, Mel. And it's barely a slump. My average is probably still in the top third of the league."

Mel eyes him. "I don't care about slumps. And yes, your average is fine."

"So what's the problem?"

Mel raises his eyebrows as if to say, *Really?* "You know damn well what the problem is."

Bryce does.

"I'm just blowing off a little steam. Things are a bit...well. You know."

"I actually don't know. Best part is I don't care."

"Come on, Mel."

Mel stands up.

Here we go.

But instead of shouting, he walks to the adjacent wall and gazes at an old black and white photo.

"They call the 1927 Yankees the greatest ball team in history."

Bryce knows this. Every ballplayer knows this. "Having Babe Ruth and Lou Gehrig helps."

Mel turns around. "There. Right there. That's the problem."

"What? Those guys were superstars. Home-run kings." Mel shakes his head sadly. "Never mind, son."

"*What?*"

Mel stands behind the desk. All business now. He slides a sheet of paper across the desk to Bryce.

Bryce looks at it. Picks it up. Puts it back down. "No," Bryce says, firmly.

Mel is silent.

"No." This time it sounds more like pleading. "Come on," Bryce says.

His stomach drops like a sinking pitch.

There it is, sports fans, Bryce Clark, once a rising star, is being sent back to the minors.

"Mel. Please. I'm 32. If you send me back now, I'll never get back."

"It's not personal Bryce."

"It's personal to me! I have a *baby* on the way. I need this."

Mel is stone-faced. Bryce feels his face flush. Anger replacing shock. "Yeah? You know what? You need *me*, Mel. I help fill those stands."

Mel shakes his head again.

"I'm about to give you a gift, Bryce. Not because I owe you, but because I like you. I haven't signed this yet. But I will. This Saturday. And then it's over. I'll let you finish out the week with the team. Let you sort things out with Stefania."

Bryce hasn't even considered how to tell Stefania. *What will she think?*

Mel sits down, begins moving paper around. The meeting is over.

The decision is made.

Bryce stands up. His legs feel weak. Shaky. *The last of last night*, he thinks.

But he knows better.

As he heads for the door, Mel speaks.

"Clean yourself up before the rest of the guys get here."

Bryce walks out the door, down the hall, and wonders just how everything could have gone so bad, so fast.

CHAPTER 2

THE GHOST OF DRAGON PARK

By the time practice starts that morning, Bryce is still wondering about the same thing. Sent back to the minors? How did it come to this?

By afternoon, he's wondering about almost everything. Are the guys looking at him strangely? Are they talking about him? Do they even like him?

I was the best of the best, he thinks. Wasn't he?

Somehow, he manages to get through practice. He stands in the locker room after everyone has left. Still in uniform, he stares at his locker. Unable to take the jersey off and unable to leave.

But he has to leave. He needs to talk to Stefania. They need to talk.

Instead, he pulls his phone from the top shelf and texts her:

Staying late for a team meeting.
Don't wait up. XO.

Bryce hopes she'll forgive him for yet another missed evening. Sadly, he knows she will.

Just as she knows there's no team meeting.

Night falls on Dragon Field.

As the cool of the evening begins to settle, Bryce has left the locker room (and that dent in the locker that seems to be judging him every time he passes it) and retreated to his second favorite place in the park, the stands.

He's always loved it here. He can remember his first time like it was yesterday. Walking through the tunnel with his father, emerging into the roar and chaos of the massive bleachers with the ball diamond laid out before him.

It was impossibly green then. Enormous, bright, and filled with excitement. Filled with potential. Anything could happen on that field.

Now, as the sun sets, the stands are empty and the field has become something darker. Somehow Bryce has gone from a world of possibility to what feels like the depths of despair.

Barely aware that he's doing it, Bryce twists the cap off the bottle in his hand and drinks.

It's the bottom of the ninth, says the voice in his head. And it looks like this game is all but over.

When the stadium lights come on, Bryce has no idea what time it is. It's dark, that much he can tell. Squinting in the glare of the light towers, he looks at his watch. Midnight.

What the hell? Other than evening maintenance and home games, those lights are never on after dark. And certainly never at midnight. There's a loud clunk.

The massive scoreboard towering over the field lights up:

Home: zero Visitor: zero
Inning: zero Outs: zero Strike: zero Ball: zero

Zeroes all around.

Bryce sits up from his slump in the bleacher seat. Something clatters beside him. An empty bottle. He bends to pick it up.

"You mind, pal?"

The voice from behind him startles him so badly he drops the bottle again. Bryce stands and spins around.

Sitting directly behind him, a few rows back, is an older man in a tweed suit.

"Hiya Bryce," he says. The accent is thick Brooklyn, the sound of a lifetime in New York.

"Do I know you?"

The man stands. He's short. Very short. He must be in his sixties, Bryce thinks. But despite his age and size, he gracefully hops the two rows of bleachers that separate them and sticks out his hand.

"Kip Jones. People call me Spooky."

Realization hits Bryce. "Look, I'm not really into doing an interview right now. On or off the record."

"I wouldn't be either if I was in your shoes." He says either like *eyedah*.

"I appreciate your understanding," Bryce says, then turns to go. "Whaddya gonna do now?" the man asks.

"I'm heading home," Bryce says.

"Nah. You know what I mean. Whaddya gonna *do* now."
"Look, Mister...Jones."

"Spooky."

"Right. Look. I've been polite. But I'm really not up for the press right now." Bryce starts walking down the concrete steps.

"Lucky for you, kid, I ain't the press. They'd have a field day with you being sent back." Bryce stops.

"How do you...never mind. Whoever you are, have a great night."

"Hard to believe," the man calls after him.

Bryce keeps walking.

"The great Bryce Holloway walking out in the bottom of the ninth."

Before he can stop himself, a lifetime of habit kicks in and Bryce's eyes move to the giant scoreboard. His mouth falls open and he freezes in place.

The board is *changing.*

The numbers, which were all zeroes, have begun to flicker and dance, spinning like the digits of a slot machine. Outs, strikes, balls, scores, they all whirl into dazzling blurs of red light, then begin to slow and then stop altogether. The board now reads:

Inning: ninth
Out: two
Strike: two
Ball: three

A full count in the bottom of the ninth, says the voice in his head. *This, sports fans, is when legends are made.*

Bryce turns around. "Nice trick," he says. "How'd you do it?"

"Trade secret," the man in the tweed suit says. "But I'll tell you what: you hit a couple of balls with me and maybe you'll see how things work."

Well, sports fans, the voice chimes in, *it looks like Bryce Holloway has finally lost not only his mojo, but his mind.*

It's true. It must be true. The booze, the stress, whatever it is, Bryce is losing it.

He shakes his head. "What is this, Field of Dreams? You going to bring some old guys out of a cornfield now?"

"This ain't magic, kid. This is just me and you having a conversation."

Why does it feel like I'm talking to the Godfather here?

"A conversation." Bryce hopes the skepticism comes across.

"Yeah. You remember those, right? We say things to each other. You say stuff and I listen. Then we switch."

Bryce looks up at the scoreboard again. Bottom of the ninth. *What the hell,* he thinks.

"Okay," Bryce says. "I'll go first. Today I got fired. I'm headed to the minors. It's all over."

"Mmmm."

"What's that mean?"

"That's my listening sound. It's supposed to make you feel validated. Heard."

"It's not working."

For the first time, Spooky smiles. A broad, sincere grin. And strangely now Bryce does feel heard.

"Lemme ask you something," Spooky says. He pronounces ask like *axe*. "Why are you sayin' it's all over?"

"Because they're sending me down. I'm finished."

"So you've been sent down?"

"That's what I'm telling you. The GM called me in this morning to tell me."

"When do you leave?"

"I don't know. The paperwork isn't--" Bryce breaks off. *What did Mel say exactly?* Spooky watches him.

"I guess I have a week left."

"Ahhh."

"Is that a listening sound?"

"That's a thinking sound. Like I'm thinking something that you aren't."

Bryce looks at this strange, small man in the suit. "That's not very reassuring."

Spooky grins again. "I like you, kid. This is going to be great."

"What's going to be great?"

Spooky continues as if Bryce hasn't even spoken. "You ever think that maybe Mel wasn't so much sending you down as he was lifting you up?"

Bryce stares out at the brilliant green of the field. He hadn't considered this.

"What are you saying?"

"I dunno, kid. What am I saying?"

"That he's giving me a chance?"

Spooky cocks his head a little. Shrugs. And then gets up and begins to walk down the hard stadium steps to the field below.

Bryce's mind begins to spin. Could it be true that it wasn't over? Is there still a chance?

"Hey," he calls after Spooky. "What do you know about this? Are you working for Mel?"

The man in the tweed suit is halfway down the stands now.

He stops and turns.

"Kid!" he calls out. "You gonna stand there or you gonna play ball?"

This is crazy, Bryce thinks. *I'm crazy.*

He watches the odd little man stepping lightly down the stadium steps.

But if so, what have I got to lose?

Bryce stands up, steps over the bottle without even realizing it, and follows the man in the tweed suit to the field below.

CHAPTER 3

THE FIRST PITCH

As he emerges from the tunnel into the brilliant green of the field, Bryce sees that the man in the tweed suit now holds a bat.

Where did that come from? For the first time, Bryce begins to wonder if this guy might be dangerous. "Look...mister. Are you even supposed to be here? I mean--"

"Are you? Remains to be seen, I'd say. And call me Spooky."

Spooky flips the bat deftly in the air, grabs it at its midpoint, and tosses it to Bryce. "Here, kid. Hit for me."

"Hit for you." Is *he* kidding?

"Humor me." He takes off his tweed coat, folds it neatly, and places it on the turf.

Seemingly from nowhere, Spooky produces a ball and tosses it to Bryce, who snatches it out of the air with one hand.

The ball is old. Like *old.* Scuffed and dirty to the point that if it was ever white, you certainly can't tell now. It's a ragged, mottled brown and Bryce can see that the stitches, a far cry from their original red, are loose and torn in places. The whole cover of the ball looks one solid hit away from falling clear off.

"You want me to hit this?"

"You afraid you can't?"

And, just like that, Bryce has had enough. The frustration, the worry, the shame--they all fall away in a rush of competitive spirit.

"Fine. Fine. I suggest then, *Spooky*, that you might wanna move back."

A grin appears on the man's face. "Attaboy, kid!"

"Like all the way back."

Spooky doesn't budge.

Fine, Bryce thinks. *I'm going to knock the cover right off this damn--*

Bryce looks down at the ball in his hand, then pauses.

Is it whiter? Less...old? No, the ball isn't whiter, but Bryce would swear the stitching is. . .*glowing.* Just faintly. Like a smear of gold around the loose threads.

"Come on, kid. I'm not getting any younger over here." Bryce blinks and shakes his head.

Fine, Bryce thinks. *No more crazy. I hit the ball, then I get out of here and get home to Stefania.*

Bryce grips the bat with one hand and tosses the ball up in the air with the other. It's a movement he's done a million times. Since before he can remember. Force of habit.

But as the ball approaches its highest point, Bryce can clearly tell that there really *is* something odd about it. The stitches are more than glowing; they're *shining.* A warm gold light is seeping out around the edges, sending tiny golden rays out in every direction.

What the hell?

Bryce has a moment to think, I should stop.

But it's all ritual now, decades of habit and muscle memory.

And before he can stop himself or wonder why an ancient baseball is glowing like a tiny sun, Bryce connects to the ball with all the power of a locomotive.

THOK

And everything goes black.

CHAPTER 4

O-U-T SPELLS OUT

Bryce opens his eyes just as a baseball flashes past him in a blur, narrowly missing his head.

He staggers back, nearly falling.

What the hell?

Laughter erupts from behind him and Bryce spins around.

A blazing light blinds him and Bryce squints trying to see the source of the laughter. Why are the field lights so bright?

But it's not the field lights. It's the *sun.*

Just moments ago he was standing in the semi-darkness of Dragon Park. Now he's staggering under a blazing sun.

"Strike," says a boy's voice.

Bryce shades his eyes, then blinks to clear the spots. To his shock, a catcher and an umpire stand behind him. The catcher is just a young boy and the ump a grown man who is sweating profusely in a black jacket and pants.

The ump, Bryce can tell, is trying not to laugh. The catcher is making no such effort. "Strike," the boy says again, grinning through his mask.

The ump cuffs the boy in the head. "I'll make the calls, thank you," he says. Undaunted, the catcher pulls the ball from his glove and smirks at Bryce and tosses it past him, back toward the mound.

Bryce looks past the catcher, where a worn chain-link backstop separates the ragged ball diamond from a latticework of old wooden bleachers. Then he spins a full circle.

It can't be.

Bryce is in Roarke County. He's standing on red clay holding a bat while staring at the dusty, tired ballpark of his youth.

Another round of chuckles ripples through the hot air and Bryce sees that the sun-beaten bleachers are almost full, packed to the brim. Men in work clothes, women in flowery sundresses. A smattering of kids is clambering about beneath the bleachers. Many of the adult's fan themselves in the heat, some even have umbrellas for shade. The whole things feels...retro? That's the word that jumps into his mind. Retro.

And hot. So hot. The sun is burning his forehead and Bryce feels the sweat begin to bead. And that's when it hits him: *this is my dream.* The same one from this morning. It's *all* a dream. A dream within a dream. Spooky, the ball, and now this. It's all a dream made more real, and stranger, by some combination of stress and exhaustion.

And let's not forget alcohol, says the annoying broadcaster in his mind.

"Let's go, son," says the umpire.

Bryce turns his gaze from the bleachers back to the ump who's watching him with something close to boredom. The catcher is still grinning as if Bryce is the funniest thing he's ever seen.

It's all a dream.

"O-U-T spells *out*," calls out a man from the stands. He's shushed by a female voice.

"Move it, son," says the ump, a little more forcefully. The catcher's grin widens even further.

It must be a dream because Bryce simply does what he's told, as if he's not even in charge of his own body. He steps into the batter's box and lines up beside the plate. He looks down to dig in his cleats and *his feet*! They're...well, they're *tiny*. And it's only now that he notices just how strange his body feels. Young. Almost vibrating with energy.

My God, I feel like I could run a marathon.

He grips the bat, a man-boy in a dream, and turns to face the pitcher.

And now he's sure he's dreaming, because the boy at the mound is Alan, his childhood rival.

Alan stares expressionlessly, watching the catcher. He lifts the glove to his midsection, and instinctively, Bryce tightens his grip and takes a breath.

The pitcher winds up and releases.

Bryce uncoils the bat from his shoulder, releasing it like a spring. Putting all the power of his body behind the tapered piece of ash. Even as the bat moves, he's already listening again waiting for that solid, perfect *thok* of a ball meeting bat.

What he gets instead is more subdued-- the brisk, efficient *thwap* of the ball hitting the catcher's glove. The sound of failure.

"Strike three! You're out." The ump says the last part almost apologetically as another round of chuckles ripples across the stand.

Bryce takes a last look at Alan, who stares impassively from the mound. Then he turns, bat in hand, and walks toward the chained-off bench that passes for a dugout.

"O-U-T, Holloway," the catcher says gleefully. "Look it up."

Now instead of yearning to hear, instead of feeling that sense of almost *leaning* with his ears, Bryce wishes he were deaf.

He barely finishes the thought before taunts begin. "Nice one, Holloway! You bat like you read!"

"O-U-T loser. That spells OUT." He feels his ears burn.

His dismay at striking out is replaced by a flash of confusion, then wonder as he sees the line of boys riding the pine behind the chain-link barrier. *Tommy? Is that Tommy? And Fletch?*

His eyes run down the length of the bench. It *is* them. All of them. The entire little-league team of his early teens. All of them still perfectly youthful, perfectly frozen in time, looking just as they were more than two decades ago.

And just like two decades ago, they're staring at him with reproach.

His eyes slide along the pink-cheeked young faces to the end of the bench. Standing there, his ball cap pulled low and wearing his coach's windbreaker despite the oppressive heat, is a tall, narrow-shouldered man.

And in that moment, Bryce forgets that he's dreaming. Or not dreaming. It doesn't matter. He forgets Spooky, Mel and what has become the dismal final week of his baseball career.

He forgets all of that, because the feeling of love, nostalgia, and loss that floods through Bryce in that moment is so strong he nearly begins to cry.

The man is Coach Teller.

The field is empty now. The sun has settled low, but the heat is just as intense. The players, the fans, and the cars that had lined the dirt lot bordering the diamond--they're all gone.

Bryce sits on the rough pine bench staring at the red earth. *This is the longest dream ever*, he thinks. And the lousiest.

He can feel Coach Teller nearby. Not talking, just...near.

"They all hate me," Bryce finally says. His voice comes out in a high, breaking warble. *Is that me?*

Coach Teller doesn't reply.

"It's the same in class," Bryce continues, the words beginning to spill out, now. "They call me retard." He can feel his throat constricting and his eyes watering. Even now, in a dream, the feelings are as strong as they were at thirteen.

Coach Teller says two words: "Follow me."

Bryce stands up, and for a moment his shame is forgotten as he marvels again over just how *amazing* he feels. His young legs are strong. He feels like he could leap right over the chain-link fence in a bound.

Maybe I should just never wake up, he thinks. But then he recalls the taunts, the classroom embarrassments, the bullying, and he knows better. Confused, energized, and saddened all at once, he simply follows his beloved childhood coach out of the bullpen and onto the field.

Coach Teller leads him to home plate and hands him a bat. Bryce grabs the narrow end, but the coach doesn't release his grip. He just keeps holding it in his long, strong fingers.

Bryce looks up at him, unsure.

"What's your job?" Coach Teller asks him. "To hit the ball."

"No. Try again."

"To get a home run." "Wrong. That's two strikes."

This is turning into dream nonsense, Bryce thinks. "A...a line drive?" he offers, weakly.

"Wrong," Coach Teller says patiently, "Your job is to *get on base*."

Bryce considers this, his thirty-two-year-old mind churning inside his young body.

"Okay. But I have to hit the ball to get on base."

"Perhaps. But hitting a ball also means you could foul. Or you could pop up and get out."

The two stand there still gripping the bat.

"Your job is to get on base," the coach repeats. "If no one ever gets on base, a team can never win."

"I don't understand," Bryce says. "What am I supposed to do?"

"It's about what you have to *not* do, Bryce. You know why you get beat by that curveball? You're swinging so hard, so fast, and so crazy, that a kid in diapers could slide a ball past you. These guys all know that. They throw you a fair, straight pitch and sure, you can knock it out of the park. You have a big bat for your age. The problem is that you can't hit anything, but a straight fair pitch and that just isn't baseball. It's not *life*."

"I just want to..." He trails off. *Hear the sound*, he thinks.

"I know. You just want to hit it out of the park. The fans love that.

People love home runs and epic stories. But, that's not how the game really works. It's a game of small steps. Little victories. You get me?"

"I think so."

"Don't think so. Be sure, son. If you're not trying to win small, then you're trying to win big. You're going for the home run. That's high risk. That's the lottery. That's your ego playing instead of you. You know what ego is?"

Bryce does. At least, the adult part of him does. But how do you explain that to a young man in a dream?

Coach Teller continues. "Your ego is the part of you that gets hurt. That's afraid that you're not good enough. At school. Out here in the field. You want to know why the curveball really beat you?"

Bryce isn't sure he does, but he's too transfixed to speak.

"The answer is that it didn't beat you. *You* did. Your ego did. Because a curveball loves the part of you that's afraid. It loves your ego."

Coach pushes the bat gently toward Bryce.

"Your ego will beat you, son. You need to take it one base at a time. You need to let go of the home run and just *get on base.* Can you do that?"

Bryce stands there, still gripping the bat, connected to his long-dead coach by the smooth taper of worn ash.

"I think so."

"Then do it. Let go."

Bryce looks at the bat, then back at Coach Teller.

"Just let go," he repeats.

Bryce drops the bat.

And the heat, the dust, Coach Teller, and finally the light itself, fade away to black.

CHAPTER 5

FIRST BASE

When Bryce opens his eyes, he's back in the stands at Dragon Park--halfway up to the nosebleed seats, exactly where he started the night. He looks down. The bottle sits beside him.

Was it really all just a dream?

More like a dream inside a dream. First the mysterious Spooky. Then Coach Teller! A lump builds in his throat. It has been years since he's even thought of the man. Now it is as if he's just spent the after- noon with him.

Which is crazy. Isn't it? It *is* crazy, right?

Let go, son. Just get on base.

He can still hear Coach Teller's even, reassuring voice in his ear. For a dream, it was incredibly detailed. So real.

And suddenly new memories rise in his mind. Of practice after practice, Coach Teller reminding him to just focus on getting on base. "One base at a time," he'd say. "One base at a time."

Extra sessions after school, with the lanky Coach pitching to him, forcing him to curb his swing. "You can't get to home without touching each base," the Coach would admonish him.

How could I have forgotten that? All that extra work?

And then he realizes what he never did at thirteen: that his coach wasn't just curbing his swing, he was curbing his *anger.*

For years Bryce struggled to read. His teacher, his parents, the special therapist they'd brought in to help, they'd *all* said the same thing: stop trying to be perfect. Just focus on the single letters. The sounds.

But he couldn't stop. He'd kept trying to read harder and harder things. Bigger books. When he got stuck, he'd double down and try even harder. It was in his nature. But all he did was fall further behind.

Yet, Coach Teller's baseball wisdom had slipped into his teen mind and spread like a sneaky virus. *One base at a time.* And as he had finally embraced the goal of just getting on base instead of trying to knock every pitch out of the park he began, without even realizing it, to change his approach to reading and writing. He went back to basics. His goal changed. Instead of trying to read huge words, he focused on small pieces. The incremental phonetics of the language. In Coach Teller's words, he started to get on base in *school.*

And, to Bryce's shock (and delight), he'd started to hit more home runs. One base had turned into two. Into three. And onward.

Bryce looked up. A faint glow is building behind the edge of the stadium walls. It's almost dawn, he realizes. *Today is going to be a very long day.* He knows he'll be exhausted by afternoon.

But he doesn't feel exhausted. He doesn't feel tired at all. For the first time in months, he feels energized.

Bryce looks down at cracked beer bottle at his feet like it's an artifact from another civilization. He steps over it and walks down the stadium steps.

Bryce emerges for the second time that night onto the green and red of the ball diamond. *Is it the second time?* he wonders. He's positive he's awake now. Well...almost positive. But he knows one thing for sure: he feels more awake than he's been in a long time.

He scans the field from left to right, taking in the grass and the empty stands.

A small figure stands at first base.

No way.

"Kid!" Spooky calls out. "Come on over." Bryce stands in

place stunned.

Yes, sports fans, says the voice. *This is a moment of truth for Bryce Holloway. It's decision time. Go or no go? Crazy or sane?*

Bryce shakes his head. *How can it be? How can any of this be real?* But there he is--a tiny man in a tweed suit looking very real and waving at him. Bryce pauses, just for a moment, long enough to wonder one last time if he truly has lost his mind.

Then he simply gives in to the crazy dream and walks toward first base. Spooky is standing just off the base gazing around the stadium. "What is happening to me?" Bryce asks.

Spooky continues to gaze about and finally replies. "There's a lot of history in these parks. An energy. A lot of hardship, but a lot of triumph. Some real tough guys came through here, kid. Real history."

Bryce follows Spooky's gaze around the vast, empty stadium.

What if my history ends here?

Spooky is silent, as if waiting for Bryce to speak. Am I really looking at the end of baseball?

Bryce finally speaks. "They say, "When the going gets tough, the tough get going," but they never tell you exactly where they get going *to.* They never tell you what to do when things fall apart."

Spooky's gaze leaves the vast open space and settles on Bryce. "Back in the day," Spooky says, "guys would hit a slump, we just accepted it. Call it math, call it chance, call it life. Fuggedabout it, I say."

"Easier said than done when your whole life is spiralling down the drain," Bryce replies. "I need to know what to do."

Spooky grins. "That saying about the tough getting going. In my day, they called that *grit.* It wasn't something you did: it was something you *had.* It was what you were made of."

"I guess I'm made of something different."

"Ahhh."

"What?"

"Kid. Forget the drama. There's nuthin' wrong with you. You're facing *adversity*. It's normal. It's baseball. It's life."

"That's not helping. I need to make a plan."

"When you're facing adversity, you don't to know what to do. You don't need me to tell you what to do."

"Then why are you here?"

"All this time kid, you've *already* known what to do. You have grit. You've already learned how to rise to a challenge by the simple fact of living your life."

"If that's true, why does it seem so hard?"

"Because," Spooky says. "You don't need to *learn* what to do. You need to remember."

Bryce looks at him. Cocks his head as if Spooky has just said some- thing he's never considered.

"That's my job," says Spooky. "Not to teach you. To help you remember."

And with that, he walks away into the outfield, leaving Bryce standing at first base with his mouth gaping open.

Spooky has almost reached the outfield wall by the time Bryce trots up behind him. The little man is staring at the high concrete barrier that separates the stands from the field.

"You know, kid," he muses. "Back in the day, a home run was a rare event. The parks were different then. The balls were different. It was a different game."

"That was Babe Ruth's time," Bryce says. "They called it the dead ball era."

"That's right. In those times, guys weren't so focused on knocking the ball out of the park--although the Babe sure did it enough. But mostly, they knew it was unlikely. Baseball then was *inside* ball. A lot more action in the infield. Do you ever wonder what guys were thinking when they stepped up to bat back then?"

Bryce has never considered this. What *were* they thinking?

"What did Coach Teller teach you?" Spooky asks.

Bryce thinks back to his dream-within-a-dream. *One base at a time.* "He told me to just get on base."

"Exactly," Spooky says. "And that's what the guys were thinking then. Just get on base."

Spooky begins to walk back toward first base and the two men stride in silence.

As they arrive at first base again, Spooky reaches in his pocket and pulls out the stained, ragged baseball Bryce had hit earlier.

"Every pitch," he says, turning the ball in his hand, "is a little bit of adversity. It's part of the game."

"I never thought of it that way."

"Trying to smack every single one of those pitches--every bit of adversity--out of the park is like a lottery. The best hitters in history-- even the Babe--strike out most of the time. The home-run odds are against you."

"You can't hit them if you don't swing."

"True words, kid, true words. But here's the thing. Lotteries are for losers. Sports betting is for chumps. If you keep swinging for home runs--for lottery wins--you'll never make it. When the pressure rises-- when you face a challenge, like right now--a huge goal like a grand slam just raises the stakes. And that's when you choke."

"So what am I supposed to do? Just wave the bat around a little and go back to the bench?"

"Momentum, kid," Spooky says.

Spooky looks toward home plate. "It's 30 yards from that plate to here. It's another 30 to second. Same to third and home. In total, you need to move 120 yards to get a run. And *runs*, kid, are what win the game. Not home runs. Just *runs*. And in this glorious game, you absolutely cannot score runs without moving around the bases."

"That's what Coach Teller told me."

"Right. Wise man. So here's the thing: life is no different, kid. When adversity comes along--which it always does--you need to think, "What's my smallest next step? In baseball, that's getting right here."

Spooky taps the base with his foot. "First base."

"First base," Bryce repeats. His mind is starting to tick.

Spooky reaches out and places the old baseball in Bryce's hand.

"Read it," he says.

Bryce looks down. In the space between the torn stitches, writing has appeared, dark against the old leather of the ball:

One base at a time.

Bryce looks up at Spooky.

"Let me be clear," says Spooky. "I'm not suggesting you never hit a home run or never win a game. What I'm telling you is that when trouble comes knocking," he looks Bryce in the eye, "like it is right now, you need to tackle that adversity one step at a time. You need to change your perspective on what you're trying to accomplish."

"I just feel like I need to redeem myself. Show what I can do. Get my mojo back."

"That's your ego talking. Adversity loves your ego," Spooky says. "Because your ego is going to keep you swinging for the stands instead of trying to get right here," he taps his foot again against first. "To the next base."

"Couldn't a little ego be...helpful? Motivate me?"

Spooky considers this. "Slippery slope, kid. Ego can be great when things are going well, but it's a disaster when adversity comes along. Then you go from confident to afraid. From home runs to strikeouts."

Bryce thinks back to Coach Teller. *What had he said? A curveball loves the part of you that's afraid.*

"When your backs against the wall," the little man continues, "getting your back up ain't gonna help. Just concentrate on moving one small step forward."

"One base at a time?" Bryce says. "One base at a time."

In that moment, it is as if something lifts from Bryce's shoulders just a little. A loosening. A lightening.

I don't want this dream to end, he thinks.

"Let's hit another," Bryce says eagerly. He turns to head toward home plate. "Go home, kid. Kiss your wife. Get some sleep."

Stefania! He'd completely forgotten. The good feeling evaporates, like mist.

"I gotta go," Bryce says, turning back to Spooky. But the little man in the tweed suit is gone.

Bryce stands alone staring across the vast field of green. And that's when it finally hits him:

I'm not dreaming.

SPOOKY'S RULES

1. One base at a time.

CHAPTER 6

STEFANIA

Bryce ignores the speed limit, driving his ruby red Lamborghini on the pre-dawn streets as fast as he dares. The glow on the horizon is turning into daybreak as he reaches his condo building. His mind is racing.

Bryce hits the button in the elevator marked "Penthouse" and feels a further stab of guilt. Stefania has been wanting to move for months.

"I want the baby to have an… *ouse*," she's said. "With a yard."

He loves her voice. The Italian accent. The "baby" as *bébé*.

He loves *her* but every time she brings up the move, he makes vague promises, pleads busyness and then does nothing. He likes the condo. Likes the idea of being at the top in the penthouse. Only the best will do.

His hand moves to his jacket pocket. He feels the lump and pulls out the aging baseball. He stares at it willing it to vanish and willing himself to wake up.

Nothing.

The elevator slows to a halt. The doors open. Same hallway. Same condo door.

"I'm really awake," Bryce says.

And then thinks, *Stefania is going to kill me.*

The good news is that Stefania is asleep.

Of course, she's asleep you idiot. It's like the crack of dawn.

The bad news is that this gives Bryce no chance to explain or apologize. Or grovel, for that matter.

He grabs a quick shower and a change of clothes in the spare room (*your room*, the broadcaster says, which he hates to admit is pretty much true) and then tiptoes to the kitchen in his bare feet to retrieve his coat.

He can feel the baseball in his pocket and he pulls it out once more.

There's no glow. No rays of golden light. No magic. It's just a dirty old baseball.

But as he spins it in his fingers, he notices the words are still there: *One base at a time.*

He thinks back to something Spooky said that night. *You ever think that maybe Mel wasn't so much sending you down as he was lifting you up?*

Could it really be true? Was there a chance to fix all of this? He

still remembers how he met Stefania. He was on a well-deserved vacation enjoying the balmy weather in Southern Italy during the offseason. All of a sudden, he found himself transfixed by her soft, melodic voice as she approached him along the Positano seafront promenade. Tanned skin, glistening in the afternoon sun. Lilac bathing suit hugging her curves.

Now, five years and a thousand putting-up-with-his-shits later, they were going to have a baby. Which necessitated the need for more space.

He pads back across the living room and climbs into the spare room bed. He tells himself that he just sleeps here to let Stefania get her rest. *But sports fans know better*, says the voice in his head.

He has just enough energy to mutter, "Shut up." Then he falls asleep with the baseball in his hand.

CHAPTER 7

THE SECOND PITCH

Bryce is the first man on the field for morning practice.

Remember when you were always the first guy on the field? he wonders.

When did that stop?

The surprised looks of the other players as they emerge to find Bryce already warming up tells him that it wasn't recently.

That's okay. One base at a time.

The morning practice goes...not bad. He's a little short on sleep--a lot short, really--but he does okay. Not being hungover certainly helps. He's on his game and it feels good.

But there's a sense of "dead man walking" in the air. He can feel it.

Sports fans, it looks like word of Bryce Holloway's impending demise is on the street.

Still, the hours pass. He has moments of hope and moments of

despair. But mostly, the morning just passes in an awkward, "Why is this guy still here?" kind of way.

And why am I still here? Bryce wonders. But he knows why: it's to try to grab a second chance. To pull a little forgiveness out of the air like a fly ball high on the back wall.

That, sports fans, is a risky play!

And that, Bryce agrees, is true.

As the morning becomes afternoon, the events of the night before begin to feel less and less real.

Did I really travel back in time? Did I meet a--

A what exactly? A ghost?

He has no idea, but by the end of the day Bryce practically sprints to the locker room, not to escape the awkward small talk of his team- mates, but to reassure himself that maybe, just maybe, he's not crazy.

He hurries to his locker, and fumbles through his jacket pocket. Sure enough, there it is. The worn baseball. He looks down the row to the dent in the locker that he'd made less than 36 hours ago. Then he looks back at the ball.

Weird magic baseball. Drunken dent in locker. It feels like a choice.

It's decision time, sports fans.

By nightfall, Bryce's mind is made up.

If he's honest with himself--something that he's coming to realize he really hasn't done much of lately--Bryce isn't quite sure exactly what he's doing. In the light of day, the events of the night before feel like at best a dream, and at worst, the first signs of him coming mentally unhinged.

But he is sure of one thing: he doesn't feel worse.

And in related news, sports fans, says the mental broadcaster, *you're also stone-cold sober.*

Regardless, he's made his choice.

He enters the stadium about halfway up--the lower half of the upper deck. It's where he'd sat the night before. But the seats are empty. Too restless to sit and wait (and too afraid he'll get thirsty) Bryce wanders back down to ground level and takes the tunnel out to the field.

The lights are out. The scoreboard is dark. If there was any magic in this place, it's gone now.

Magic, he thinks. *Is that really what it was?*

He reaches into his pocket and pulls out the baseball. It looks, well, ordinary. Just like everything else.

Bryce absently flips the ball from hand to hand as he scans the field and the stands hoping to see Spooky.

On his second visual lap of Dragon Field, his eye catches on a rack near the home dugout where a single, lonely bat stands upright.

Those racks are supposed to be empty, he thinks, and he walks toward the dugout. It looks strangely ominous--a gaping, dark mouth beneath the seats.

"Hello?" he calls. "Spooky?"

Why, yes, sports fans, it IS a little spooky, says the voice in his head. "Shut up," Bryce mutters.

He snatches the bat from the rack, a little embarrassed by the way his heart has begun to race just a little, and then beats a somewhat hasty retreat away from the dugout toward home plate.

Things feel a little less ominous here away from the dugout. He kicks his shoes into the dirt beside the plate, rests the bat on his shoulder, and pulls the tired old baseball from his jacket pocket.

Bryce tightens his grip on the bat, but then feels a strange reluctance overcome him. It's as if he doesn't *want* to hit the ball. Doesn't want to it to fly off into the darkness of the outfield never to be seen again.

He loosens his grip on the bat.

There's a *sizzling* sound and the giant scoreboard above the field comes to life.

STRIKE: one

"Hey," Bryce says. "I haven't even done anything yet."

Silence. Bryce looks down at the ball in his hand. *Okay. I get it.*

"Well, old-timer," he says. "Let's send you off right, shall we?"

With practiced casualness, he tosses the ball in the air and grips the bat to swing.

By the time the ball reaches its zenith, the stitches have begun to glow.

By the time it drops back toward the hit zone, it's a tiny, glowing sun once more and Bryce connects with it dead-center as if it were a mile across.

Thok!

CHAPTER 8

THE FALL

Even before Bryce opens his eyes, he knows that Dragon Field is gone. The sprawling green, the stadium walls, the stands--he can tell just by listening that they're all gone. The wide-open feeling of physical space has been replaced with something *close.*

Bryce opens his eyes. He's standing in a bedroom--a small but bright second-floor room with the sunlight flooding in through a dormer window across a single bed and wooden dresser.

The walls are covered in baseball paraphernalia. Pennants, team posters, baseball cards. Ticket stubs and signed programs.

Bryce feels a rush of joy flood through him. He takes a breath, the smell immediately familiar.

Home.

This is his childhood bedroom, as familiar to him as his own name. It's where he dreamed, and dreamed, and dreamed some more of a life in the big leagues.

Two feelings arrive back-to-back in immediate sequence. The first one is, of all things, satisfaction.

I did it, he thinks. *Just like I dreamed in this very room. I made it big.*

The second feeling is shame.

And then I threw it away.

What, he wonders, would his teenage self think now?

But what is *now*? This room--it no longer exists. The house is gone; his parents are gone. Everything is long gone.

Where...or *when* is he?

He barely has a chance to register the thought when he hears a voice that stops his heart.

"Bryce?"

He would recognize it anywhere.

It can't be. He opens his mouth, but cannot make a sound. He is so overwhelmed with...*happiness* that he can barely stand.

"Bryce honey. The newspaper people are here. They want to talk to you."

And just like that the happiness vanishes. So suddenly, it's like it has been vacuumed from his body by some impossibly powerful force.

The voice belongs to his mother. His mother, who has been dead for a decade, and who Bryce misses terribly. It's *her*, he knows it beyond any shred of doubt and it's what has filled him with joy.

But what has erased that joy is the realization that he knows *exactly* what day it is.

Bryce spins around; his eyes searching the room wildly. He has no idea what he's looking for. He's simply overcome with the need to escape. To escape this room. To escape the men downstairs who want to ask him about today's game.

To escape what's coming next.

He paces the room like a prisoner in a cell. He Looks out the window barely registering the twenty Mercedes convertibles lining the streets and the people walking past on the sidewalk below.

Why today? He thinks. *Why now?*

He remembers every inch of these walls. He lovingly stroked the base of his high school baseball trophy, his mind reflecting back to the start of his illustrious journey. This was the time where his prodigious skills were first noticed. But then his injury happened. Memories of that day come rushing back. Bryce had just hit an inside-the-park home run and was flying around the bases. He remembered the gasp of the crowd, the look of utter horror on his coaches' faces as he slid awkwardly into third base, his knee twisting at an unusual angle, shredding parts of it.

For his half-asleep brain, it's a sound of his alarm clock. It's sound of *school* and he wishes it would stop. That school would go away. School is hard. All he wants to do is play ball. Ball is easy.

Then he wakes up, realizes where he is- where he's been for *weeks*- and Bryce knows he would give anything to be in school right now.

He's in a hospital room, with fluorescent lights irritating his eyes. He's surrounded by bright balloons, flowers, and gifts. He knows this room, and he *loathes* it at the same time.

He wildly searching gaze stops on a cherrywood chair where his tattered brown baseball glove sits with a baseball tucked into it.

His breathing slows. His old glove! Amazing. He reaches for it... But nothing happens. Nothing much, anyway. His knee and the lower part of his body aches so violently, that is makes any movement impossible.

When he'd hit the first ball with Spooky, Bryce felt as if he was thirteen years old again, and it had been a revelation. He felt incredible. Supple. Filled with energy. A coiled, unbreakable spring.

Now, he feels the opposite. A limp sense of emptiness.

The present moment crashes in with heart-wrenching news.

Full and complete tears of his MCL, ACL and various other dislocations in his knee. The doctor's prognosis is bleak- Bryce could be out for a long time, possibly a year. His career hangs in the balance.

And now he feels something new in him. It's as if all the space left behind when hope evaporated has been replaced with something new: anger. He can feel his brow knit in ever-deepening frustration.

He reaches for the ball again. His fingers clench, then fall open. He feels tears build in his eyes, and steadily roll down his cheek. "I guess your mama was right, " says a quiet voice with a slight southern drawl.

"You're Sid Mayes," he croaks, his voice rough from lack of use.

The man nods, eyes gazing around the room. It's obvious that he's uncomfortable here. His eyes flick from the IV bag to Bryce, over to Bryce's heavily bandaged knee, and then back again to Bryce.

He's powerfully built, Bryce can see. Much more so than in his rookie card, which Bryce owns. (*Whatever happened to all those cards?*) The card that shows Sid in his familiar catcher's crouch, the huge mitt opens to the camera, eyes burning with ferocious intensity. He's wearing the New York Knights jersey, a team he would return to later in his career and help power to three World Series Championships in a row.

He is one of Bryce's heroes. Bryce isn't even a catcher, but this man to Bryce is a symbol of everything the sport means.

And now to his surprise his hero is...*nervous*? "What are you doing here?"

With what seems like no small effort, Sid pulls his eyes from the

medical equipment crowding the room and looks at a spot somewhere just above Bryce's left shoulder.

"Your coach called me. Well...called a guy who knows me."

He walks further into the room, his eyes still anywhere but on Bryce.

"I talked to your mom. She's real worried about you. I told her I don't know nothin' about medicine. She said that was just fine."

Bryce nods. He understands now what he didn't at age 18: that his parents are now as worried about his mind as they are about his body. Perhaps more. Bryce's been lying in a fog of resentment and anger for weeks. He's half-heartedly tried physio, but all he can think is: *Why me?*

Sid looks about once more, as if making a decision. After what seems like some long inner struggle, he begins to speak. "I never told no one," Sid begins.

He speaks quietly, but with confidence, and Bryce realizes that what he thought was nervousness was perhaps just Sid observing him. Taking it all in. *He was figuring me out*, he thinks.

"A couple years into the majors, I got into a bit of trouble," Sid says. "I had to leave the Knights."

"I thought you wanted a series ring. That you left for a better shot." "That would be what I told everyone," he says. "But I had some trouble."

"What kind of trouble?"

"Well. You know. Cards. Maybe a little drink. You know?" Bryce did know. At least a little.

"That would have been no big deal, but I got mixed up with some...well, some wrong guys." He looks directly now at Bryce. "Don't ever play cards for money," he says quickly. Then his gaze returns to just over Bryce's shoulder.

"They gave me a real good deal, though. I still had some contract left. Coulda stayed. Coulda fought. But they let me go with a good story and a second chance."

"Good thing," Bryce says.

"Yeah? Yeah. I think it was," Sid says. "It was good."

In Bryce's mind, a strange commotion is taking place. He's reliving an actual moment in his life, but he's reliving it as an adult. He has new questions now for Sid. Questions like *how'd you kick the booze?* But instead he just asks the same question his teenage self had asked from this very bed:

"What was it like to win the World Series?"

Sid is quiet for so long that Bryce almost repeats the question. But he finally says, "I guess it was pretty great."

This answer startles Bryce. "You guess?"

Sid chuckles. "Yeah, it was great."

"What was the best part?" This time the answer comes right away. "Starting all over after I left the Knights the first time."

"That was better than winning the world series?" Sid nods. "Yeah. Yeah, it really was."

"Mr. Mayes. You hit the game-winning home run in the last game of the world series. You--*you*--won the series for the Knights. How can starting all over possibly be better than winning the world series?"

"Because that's when I learned *how* to win the world series."

Now, adult Bryce is just as rapt as he was as a child. Although he can so clearly recall Sid visiting him at the hospital, there are clearly huge gaps in his memory.

"How?" Bryce asks. Sid thinks again.

"You know, most catchers aren't great hitters."

"Yeah, but you aren't most catchers."

"I was a lousy bat just like most catchers," Sid insisted. "In fact, I was lousier than most. That's also part of why I was traded." Somehow this little fact has escaped Bryce's baseball-hungry mind.

"When they traded me to the Hawks, there was this offensive coach who..." Sid trailed off, seeming to search for the right word. "Well. He didn't really *believe* in weak hitters. He said it didn't have much to do with strength, speed, or some kind of gift."

"Really?"

"Yeah. That's about what I said."

"If it's not about that, what was it about?"

Sid thought again. "His idea was that the difference between good and bad hitters wasn't about hitting harder, it was about making better choices."

"Better *choices*?"

Sid's gaze lands on Bryce's glove and ball. He grabs the ball and holds it up.

"Every pitch is a choice. When someone throws this tiny ball at you at a hundred miles an hour, you got a decision to make: are you gonna swing or not?"

Bryce watches how Sid easily moves the ball from hand to hand. His own fingers spasm in feeble twitches and he feels tears prick his eyes.

"The pitcher is basically trying to get you to make the wrong choice. To swing when you shouldn't. To pull up short when you should swing through. They work the corners. Try to drag you out of your sweet spot and into a strike or overlook a perfect pitch right down the middle."

Sid sets the ball and glove down.

"What they taught me at the Hawks was to choose my pitches. To be patient and to wait for things in the zone. And that was most true when things were tough."

"How so?"

"When you first step up to the plate, you've got some slack. No strikes, no balls. But as the count goes up, the stakes go up. You get two strikes against you and you've got a challenge on your hands. You can't afford to mess up. Suddenly the pressure is on."

Bryce knows this all too well. How many times had he choked when the count was against him?

"I was no good with the pressure," Sid continues. "Instead of becoming more patient, I'd be jumpy as hell. You give me two strikes, and I'd swing at anything at that point. They taught me to settle down; choose my pitches. Be patient and wait for the right moment."

"So what happened?"

"I did what they told me. Hell--that was my job. And I didn't want to get traded again. I just shut my mouth and did what they said. And...well, it worked real good. My average went way up. Way up for a catcher, but way up for anyone, I suppose."

"That's how you became a great hitter? By choosing better?" "I know. It sounds obvious. I nearly laughed at the fella who told me. But when things are hard, it's the simple things you forget. Like swinging for the pitches that you can hit."

There's a light knock at the door and a nurse enters the room carrying a tray with a small vial and a syringe. Crisp white uniform and white cap. Old school, like a nurse in a movie. *Only this isn't a movie*, Bryce thinks. *It's like a movie, but...real.*

"I'm sorry sir," she says to Sid. "Visiting hours are over and this young man needs his rest."

Sid nods. "Yes'm," he says politely, but stays standing.

The nurse draws a few cc's of a clear fluid and injects it into the IV line that leads from the clear saline bag on the hook near Bryce's lower extremities. *Ow!* he thinks, absently.

Then she's gone and it's just Bryce and Sid.

"I should be going," Sid says.

"Thank you for coming," Bryce says.

Sid reaches down and plucks Bryce's ball from his glove. "Choose your pitches Bryce." He says quietly. "I can't imagine what this is like for you, but I can tell you this: *you can't hit every pitch*. Some are wide. Some are low. Some are just too darn fast. It don't matter. The point is you can't hit 'em all. Like I told your mama, I don't know much about medicine. I'm just a ballplayer. But I know that when things are hard, you gotta focus on the pitches you can hit and forget about the rest."

And with that, Bryce's boyhood hero nods, turns, and walks out of the hospital room.

Moments later Bryce's eyes grow heavy, then close, and the room grows dim.

CHAPTER 9

SECOND BASE

Bryce opens his eyes to find himself standing in the batter's box at home plate.

It feels like he's just spent hours in the hospital room in the past, yet it's as if he's just *blinked* here in the present. *What the* hell *is*--

He's interrupted by a voice. "Kid! Hey kid!"

This has to be a joke, Bryce thinks.

But if it's a joke, it's a consistent one. Bryce looks toward that Brooklyn voice and sees the man in the tweed suit standing directly across the diamond from him just a step off of second base.

Spooky tips his cap. "Come on over," he calls.

Spooky's voice doesn't exactly echo, but it carries. It *resonates* in the empty stadium. Normally there would be tens of thousands of fans and Bryce realizes it's the first time he's heard the sound of a single human voice on the field. It's odd. Unsettling.

Bryce takes a step toward second base, intending to walk right over the pitcher's mound on his way.

"Whoa there, kid. That ain't the way."

"What?"

Even from this distance, Bryce can see Spooky's wide grin.

Realization sets in. "You're kidding, right?" "One base at a time, kid."

This is ridiculous, Bryce thinks. But he drops the bat and begins a slow jog to first base.

"One base at a time," he mutters as he rounds first base and trots to second where a happily-grinning Spooky waits, his tweed coat now draped over his arm.

"Happy?" Bryce asks.

"As a clam, kid."

"I think I know what's going on here," Bryce says.

"Mmmm?" Spooky says.

"Very funny. This is, like, a shrink thing, right? Sports psychology? You're one of those brain trainers they bring in when guys are choking."

But even as the words leave his mouth, Bryce knows that isn't what this is at all. What part of sports psychology explains time travel and magical glowing baseballs?

"You done?" Spooky asks.

Bryce sighs. "I'm done. I have no idea what the hell is going on here, but I'm just going to--what do the recovering addicts say?--*let go and let God?*'

"An excellent plan."

"So now what?"

"You tell me. You just ran here from first base."

Bryce opens his hands in a *so what?* gesture.

"So what was first base?" Spooky presses.

Bryce thinks back to the writing on the ball. To Coach Teller. To the summer he was thirteen and his desperate attempts to knock every ball out the park.

No, to knock everything *out of the park*, he realizes, as the insight hits home. *The bullies, the opposingpitcher. School. Everything.*

"Just get on base," he says to Spooky. "One base at a time."
"Bingo. When you're facing adversity, you need to focus on the next smallest step. You need to make steady progress forward no matter how small the progress is."

"Right. Coach Teller taught me that."

"Did it help?"

"Sure. My batting average went up, but my scoring went up even further."

"No, kid. I mean, did it help in your *life*?"

Bryce knows where Spooky is headed with this. "Yeah. It helped me with school. With reading, writing. One base at a time. One word at a time. Baby steps, I guess. But I did that in physio too, after I got injured. I mean, at that point in time baby steps was all I *could* do. But I still struggled."

"Until?"

Bryce thinks back to his flashback. The hospital. The doctors. The nurses.

"Until Sid Mayes showed up," he says.

"And what did he say?"

"Choose your pitches," Bryce says, recalling those final moments before the medications knocked him out.

"That's it, kid. Choose your pitches. But what happened after that?" Bryce considers the question. What *did* happen? Even now the visit with Sid which had seemed so real has taken on the faded quality of a dream. Sid had visited him that day, sure. And they'd talked. And then...

A thought bubbles up from the recesses of his mind.

Bryce knows exactly what happened. He just doesn't want to say it. "What happened after that, kid?" Spooky repeats.

Bryce looks around the darkened ballpark and in a quiet voice says,

"I gave up on baseball."

"Ahhh," Spooky says.

"I know," Bryce says. "That's your thinking sound. So what are you thinking that I'm not?"

"I'm thinking the opposite of what you're thinking."

"Can we just use plain English? Please?"

Spooky cracks open his broad grin. "Look, kid. Until the day Sid showed up, you were still trying to play *baseball*. You were lying half- paralyzed in a hospital bed trying to play baseball for the love of Pete."

Bryce thinks of his hands spasming awkwardly trying to reach his ball glove.

"That was my dream," he says defensively.

Spooky lifts his head to the stadium seats. "Believe me," he says slowly, "I understand."

"Well, I sure don't."

"Don't you? You didn't give up on baseball, kid. *You picked healing your body.*"

Realization dawns on Bryce. "I was choosing my pitches," he says. "I was choosing my pitches!"

"Yeah, kid. Yeah. And what nobody told you is that at the same time, you were also choosing what to *feel*."

"What to feel?"

"When things are tough," Spooky says, "you have to choose your response. You have to choose how to feel, how to think, and as a result, how to act. But here's the magic. *Every choice you make eliminates its opposite.* You can't choose to not swing and swing at the same pitch. It's one or the other. *And the same is true for emotions.* You can't hold two opposite emotions at the same time. You can't be miserable and grateful at the same time. You can't be angry and happy."

Bryce has never considered this. *But it's true*, he thinks.

"When you chose healing over baseball, you chose hope over resentment. And then you focused on the things that healed your body."

Bryce thinks back to what happened next. The experimental treatment. The physio. The eventual recovery. *They never would have put me in that program if I'd stayed so angry. So focused on what I'd lost.*

"When adversity shows up--and it always does--you need to decide. You need to choose your battles. Do you want to be angry? Resentful? Feel sorry for yourself? Or do you want to have hope? Be grateful? Every choice you make eliminates another choice. Choose gratitude and you simply can't choose anger. Choose love and you can't choose fear. You can't hold them both at the same time."

"Choose your pitch," Bryce says.

"Why hit the sloppy slider with cockeyed spin on it?" Spooky asks. "You know odds are that you're going to foul it off. Why swing at that outside pitch? Choose your battles. Pick your pitches. Swing in your circle of competence."

Spooky reaches into his jacket pocket and pulls out the worn baseball.

"Pitchers are going to work the corners," he says. "They're trying to drag you out of your sweet spot and into a strike. And the rest of the world is going to do the same."

He tosses the ball to Bryce.

"Welcome to second base, kid."

Bryce looks down at the ball. Across the seam from the first message, a new line of writing has appeared:

Choose your pitches

Bryce looks up and Spooky is gone.

SPOOKY'S RULES

1. One base at a time.

2. Choose your pitches.

CHAPTER 10

THE NEW GUY

The next morning , Bryce stands at the locker experiencing a rare emotion: pre-game jitters.

When was the last time you were truly nervous before a game? he wonders. There was always some pre-game energy, but this was different.

He could hear the muted sounds of the stadium--so different from the night before when he'd stood there alone in the darkness. But where that sound would normally fill him with excitement, he now feels a sense of dread, as if he's about to testify before a jury of 30,000 people.

He dresses quietly and follows his team to the field.

By the third inning, Bryce's nervousness is blooming into full-blown anxiety. He's struck out at his first two at-bats. And, worse still, *not a single ball.*

What the hell is the matter with me? I'm swinging like a kid in little league.

Now, he sits in the dugout ignored by his teammates. Wishing the game was over. Wishing *everything* was over. Wishing he could just curl up with Stefania and that somehow the world would disappear.

He'd woken up that morning feeling better than he had in a while. He was excited about the game and excited about his prospects for a second chance.

Stefania had even greeted him warmly in a bear-like yet affectionate embrace, as if she could sense the shift taking place within Bryce. Or smell the lack of booze. Whatever it was, Bryce didn't care. He felt good.

"You know," he'd said to her as she handed him a cup of coffee. "We should probably start looking for a home with a little more space--for the baby."

The look on her face right then was worth a thousand penthouse condos. She hadn't said a word. Just kissed him slowly, full on the lips, and squeezed his hand tightly.

One base at a time, he'd thought. *One base at a time.*

But now, far from the quiet penthouse under the gaze of tens of thousands of screaming fans, even one base was beginning to seem impossible.

"Holloway!" a voice calls, and he's jerked from his daydream. "Get your ass on deck."

Bryce takes a few warm-up swings only half-heartedly, watching the batter before him who flies out two pitches in. Then he's up.

Bryce walks to home plate and steps into the batter's box. He shoulders the bat and looks out at the pitcher, his eyes shaded by a ball cap pulled low.

Please let me hit this.

He's not even close. Bryce watches, in slow-motion disappointment, as the curveball sails around his bat in an elegant dance.

STRIKE: one

Goddamn it! Bryce tightens his grip, feeling the anger flow into him, the adrenaline coursing through his system.

The next pitch is a fastball that has Bryce feeling like his arms are moving through molasses. *Too slow! What the hell is the matter with me?*

STRIKE: 2

Bryce steps out of the batter's box in frustration. *I have to get focused*, he thinks.

He adjusts his cap and something catches his eye. In the second row behind home plate, a man sits, calm amidst the chaos of the screaming, animated fans.

A man in a tweed suit, whose face spreads in a wide, toothy grin. He holds up a tattered-looking baseball and waggles it at Bryce.

Just get on base, Bryce thinks. *I* know. *I'm trying.*

And then, he hears a voice in his head--that familiar, thick New York accent: *Choose your pitches, kid.*

Bryce looks at Spooky, and feels the anxiety and adrenaline leave him. Feels a calm spread through his body.

He steps back into the batter's box and shoulders the bat.

Less than a minute later, and for the second time in less than 24 hours, Bryce finds himself at second base.

Yes! He thinks, giving himself a mental high-five. *One base at a time.*

Spooky's calming presence--or disarming grin; Bryce wasn't sure which had centered Bryce enough that he let the next three lousy pitches go by. As the count tipped toward Bryce, it was if he could feel the pressure shift off of him toward the pitcher. Sure enough, the next pitch was right in the sweet spot and Bryce crushed it for a double.

Choose your pitches.

To his delight, the next bat in the Dragon lineup quickly drives a single into right field, giving Bryce plenty of time to get to third.

Two bats later and he's carried home by a line drive up the center.

Well, this is an unexpected surprise, sports fans, says the inner broad- caster. *It's been a long time since hitter Bryce Holloway has made a trip to the plate the long way.*

It's true, Bryce thinks. *When was the last time I actually scored a run?* He flushes with embarrassment. Has it really gotten that bad? How long has it been? Weeks? *Months?* To his surprise, his shame vanishes as he enters the dugout to a few high-fives and even a cautious "Good run, Holloway" here and there.

It's as if he's forgotten how good it feels simply to work his way around the bases.

When did I get so addicted to home runs? he thinks.

Bryce sneaks a glance over to Mel Oscar standing in the back of the bullpen, but the man is staring out at the field, arms crossed.

Bryce's good feeling disappears.

After the initial anxiety, the rest of the game passes quickly and, to Bryce's surprise, pleasantly.

Each time he steps up to the plate, he feels the pressure of the crowd and a surge of adrenaline. He even catches himself saying, I'm going to knock this out of the park. But then he retreats to Spooky's mantras:

One base at a time.

Choose your pitches.

And it works. *Damn it, it works!*

He still strikes out twice and flies out three more times, but those outs are entirely okay in the face of the four runs that he adds to the scoreboard.

Each time at bat, Bryce tries to catch a glimpse of Spooky again, but the seat in the second row behind the plate is now occupied by a lunatic face-painter who can barely keep from spilling his beer all over his prodigious stomach.

No matter. In the end, the Dragons ride home to an 11-9 victory.

I'm making my way back, Bryce thinks.

Bryce hangs around after the game hoping to talk to Mel. He showers, takes his time, and waits for the players to clear out. *Once Mel sees me sober and hitting well, this will all be over.*

As he leaves the locker room though, he hears voices out on the field. The sound of laughter. A muted "Yeah baby!"

And the unmistakable THOK of bat against ball.

Curious, he makes his way down the player's tunnel and out into the vast stadium, which even now is still lit.

Another thok!

A small crowd has gathered at home plate--mainly guys from the team and a couple of reporters Bryce knows. He sees Mel there too, standing a little off to the side.

There's another thok as Bryce walks over to join the group followed by a "Woo!"

The group falls suddenly silent as Bryce approaches.

Uh-oh, sports fans, says the voice.

The men at home plate part briefly and Bryce catches a glimpse of a young, dark-haired man. Well-muscled, no more than 19 years old.

"Oh. Hey Bryce," says one of his teammates awkwardly. "Uh. This is Louis."

The teenager steps forward, "It's an honor to meet you, Mr. Holloway."

Bryce shakes his hand, mumbles a welcome, and steps back. Then he turns and quickly shuffles back the way he came.

The last thing Bryce hears as he leaves the stadium is the sweet sound of wood on leather that he knows, just *knows*, is a home run.

Who is that guy? Bryce wonders.

You know damn well who he is, says the voice. Yes, he does.

It seems to take hours for the last of the stadium cleaners to leave, for the big halogen lights to shut off and plunge Dragon Park into darkness.

He's already called Stefania. He told her he'd be late, but he could tell from her voice that she wasn't angry. At least not *as* angry.

"It's something I have to do," he'd told her. "Just me."

There was a pause and Bryce had realized he was holding his breath. "Be careful," she says, at last.

Bryce exhales with relief and heads for the stands.

On the way, he passes the now darkened players' lounge. Almost without realizing it, he stops and his hand reaches out to grab the ornate golden doorknob. He knows the fridge inside is well- stocked. What harm could one beer do? After all, they did win today, didn't they? *And I helped make that happen! I should be celebrating.* Then he thinks of Stefania. And Mel. And Spooky.

Choose your pitches.

He detaches his hand from the doorknob and continues down the hall.

CHAPTER 11

THE THIRD PITCH

THE STADIUM IS IN DARKNESS.

Bryce takes what he's come to think of as his usual seat in the stands. He's restless. *Do I just go down there and hit the ball? Do I wait?* A familiar voice rings out behind him. "Peanuts! Hot nuts! Roasted, salted, and guaranteed to please."

Bryce turns. It is indeed Spooky, but instead of his trademark tweed suit and hat he wears an old-fashioned concession vendor's outfit-- striped shirt and a small peaked cap. Hanging from a strap around his neck is a box filled with bags of popcorn and peanuts. He walks slowly down the stadium steps, hawking his wares.

"Get your peanuts! Hot nuts!" Bryce can't help but smile.

"What?" Spooky says. "A fella can't earn a livin'?"

"Crowd's a little thin tonight, Spooky."

"Yeah, pal. It's killin' me."

Bryce reaches in his pocket and tosses him a nickel, which Spooky snatches from the air. "What'll this get me?" Bryce asks. "My undying gratitude and a bag of peanuts, kid. Follow me." He hands Bryce a small paper bag of peanuts, then steps lightly down the stadium steps and disappears into the darkness.

Bryce looks at the bag.

Well, sports fan, says the rich broadcasting voice. *It looks like our hero might be nuts after all.*

"That's not even close to funny," Bryce says. Then cringes at his voice echoing through the stands. "And...now I'm talking to myself. *Great, Holloway. Just great.*"

He sets the peanuts down and walks down the stairs to the waiting diamond.

Bryce emerges from the dark of the tunnel relieved as the field lights come alive, turning the charcoal grey of the night diamond into brilliant green and red.

I'm still nervous, he realizes. *This guy could be anybody.*

But he knows that Spooky isn't just anybody. He's *somebody.* I just don't know who, Bryce thinks.

But whoever he is, the man is back at the pitcher's mound and back in this tweed suit.

"Now what?" Bryce calls out.

"Are you kiddin' me, kid? You wanna talk, or you wanna play ball?"

Bryce smiles, kicks his shoes into the dirt beside home plate, and raises the bat to his shoulder.

THOK

CHAPTER 12

THE CHOKE

Bryce opens his eyes. He has barely enough time to think, *I wonder where I am this time*, before he throws up, narrowly missing his shoes.

God, he thinks. *Is this some kind of...withdrawal?*

But that makes no sense. He hasn't had a drink in two days, sure, but it hasn't bothered him at all. Ten seconds ago, he felt fine. Hell, he felt great. He wasn't even missing the booze. It's almost miraculous, but he's barely noticed given how unbelievable everything else has seemed.

Booze or not, his stomach churns again and it takes several deep breaths to get the nausea under control.

He stands up straight and tries to get his bearings. He's in a parking lot, that much is clear, but he's not sure where. The whole scene, though, is vaguely familiar.

I've been here before.

He turns 180 degrees, then stops, his mouth falling open. "Wow."

The word just slips out and he knows with certainty not only where he is, but that *wow* is exactly what he would have said more than fifteen years ago when he stood in this exact spot.

And now he knows with certainty why he just threw up. It's not a virus and it's not withdrawal.

No, sports fans, says the voice, *Mr. Small-Town Big-Shot Bryce Holloway isn't sick. He's nervous.*

That, Bryce knows, is as true as a home run. He is nervous. Or is it was nervous? What was the right tense to use when you were transported back in time? Bryce has no idea. But his stomach is in knots and his legs, which should be filled with late teen energy, instead feel shaky like a morning-after hangover.

He stares across 20 acres of vacant parking lot at the monolithic stadium that dominates the horizon.

Then leans over once more and throws up in the grass.

An hour later, Bryce has reached a milestone (for the second time) that he's dreamed of since childhood: He's standing at the edge of a baseball diamond wearing the first professional baseball uniform of his life.

The jersey is that of the Pittsburgh Python, the crest an embroidered dark blue and gold Serpent coiled around a gleaming white baseball. Even now, doing this for what is effectively the second time, Bryce is struck by just how powerful the moment is. *How did I forget this?* he wonders, and thinks back fifteen years to a time when this was all new. He was still, he realizes, just a kid. But a healthy one, at least-- thanks to hard work and a near- miracle cure, he'd beaten the disease that had left him close to paralyzed.

Would you agree, sports fans? I'd say that visit from Sid Mayes had a lot to do with it.

It's true, Bryce realizes. He's never thought of it that way, but the visit from Sid had been critical in keeping Bryce focused as he slowly fought his way back to game shape.

Two years later he went first in the draft straight out of high school. It was the comeback of all comebacks, a flurry of excitement and tension that culminated in this, his first day of the majors.

And now I can barely keep my knees from knocking together, he thinks.

To be fair, there was (and apparently *is*) enormous pressure on him. He's made a name for himself as a tremendous hitter and expectations are high. Not just because he's done so well, but because he's being paid...*well, ridiculously*, Bryce thinks.

Later of course he would earn much more, but at the time he remembers it as more money than he thought he could ever spend in a lifetime.

Well, sports fans, says the voice, *that sure turned out to be a load of baloney.*

It sure did. Bryce knows now that there's no amount of money you can't spend if you put your mind to it.

And I sure put my mind to it.

But now in this moment, at eighteen years old Bryce is famous--at least in a small way--rich, and under enormous pressure.

"Holloway," hollers a voice. "Today, Holloway. Today."

Bryce looks up from his reverie to see the Python manager a short, squat man with a military-style crewcut and a red face, waving at him. "I'm getting old, here, Holloway. We're all getting old waiting to see your *wonderfulness*."

His emphatic disdain on the last word is obvious, and Bryce flushes. He's forgotten all of this. The "wonderfulness" is a play on the newspapers who called him "Wonder Kid" in the period leading up to the draft. His deal with the Pythons had been the subject of much talk.

And much criticism, he remembers. And flushes deeper as a series of chuckles roll through the dugout behind him.

God. I'd forgotten how awful this all was.

"Batter up, Holloway," says a voice from the dugout.

"Yeah," says another. "I'm fresh out of wonder. Let's see some." Bryce feels his hackles rise and he forgets that he isn't really eighteen and this scene isn't real--at least not in the sense he thinks of real-- but just some bizarre flashback. Now in the heat of the moment this is all very real and very *now.*

Little League, Big League, he fumes. It's all the same crap. He yanks a bat from the rack, spilling several others--which sends another series of chuckles through the dugout--and marches to the batter's box.

He feels the manager's eyes on him and he steps quickly to the plate with no preamble.

The pitcher at the mound sizes Bryce up, but his face is impassive. He gives away nothing.

Bryce snaps the bat to his shoulder. Nods at the pitcher. *Bring it on*, he thinks.

And he does.

He brings on a curveball the likes of which Bryce has never encountered, one that arcs so dramatically through the air that Bryce has no chance of hitting it. He swings, missing wildly, and the ball thumps solidly into the catcher's mitt.

Bryce silently curses himself, but at the same time he's flabbergasted *That curve! That ball can't be legal.*

But part of him knows it is. Part of him knows a truth he doesn't want to hear: this is the big leagues and everything is different. *Harder. Faster. Better.*

He clenches his jaw and lifts the bat to his shoulder.

This time, the catcher signals a fast ball. And it's so fast that Bryce has barely started his *swing* when it thumps into the glove behind him.

You're playing like it's your first time! His inner voice is practically screaming at him and Bryce feels his stomach tighten, the nausea threatening to rise again.

He raises the bat once more, but it's over before it begins. Bryce, determined to not be fooled yet again, lets the pitch go by. But the slider drops into the strike zone at what seems like the last moment and someone gleefully yells, "You're out" from the dugout.

Bryce turns, his face turning red, and catches sight of the squat form of the Python manager shuffling down the tunnel and off the field.

It's his first day in the major leagues and Bryce Holloway has just been struck out by his own teammate. Three pitches, three strikes.

You're out.

The rest of the day passes in a blaze of humiliation. Bryce only manages to connect once with a ball--a weak foul to left field on a pitch that he knows was a charity toss, slowed down just to let him hit something, *anything.*

By the time the afternoon ends, even the chuckles and teasing have stopped. The eyes of the older players, at first keenly watching the Wonder Kid, now just glance off him.

It's no longer just Bryce who's ashamed; it's everyone.

As practice winds down, Bryce lags behind his teammates, dawdling, avoiding the locker room. He sits alone in the dugout where, with the stadium empty, he can hear the faint sound of showers and muted conversation in the distance.

The last rays of sunshine are clearing the rim of the stadium, turning the turf a golden green. Bryce leans back against the dugout wall and closes his eyes, feels its warmth on his face. *What a disaster. Living through this a second time feels almost worse than the first.*

He's jolted to attention by the CRACK of bat against ball.

Bryce climbs slowly out of the dugout, although he already knows who he'll see.

Standing in the batter's box is a Pittsburgh Python legend.

Bryce is surprised by the man's size. He's slender for a pro ball player, almost skinny. The kind of kid who would normally get weeded out before Double-A unless he could put on twenty or thirty pounds of muscle.

But nobody weeded out DeShawn Parker. He's a good fielder, but his real skill is at the plate. Parker, Bryce knows, is perhaps the finest clutch hitter in the league, maybe in history. And right now, at the end of a long day, DeShawn Parker is *still* hitting balls. Bryce steps to the warm-up circle wanting to watch him hit, but not wanting to interrupt. But DeShawn seems to have a sixth sense. He turns around and raises a hand in acknowledgment, then smacks another ball into right field.

Bryce walks to the batter's box, amazed that he remembers this awful day as clearly as ever, but has little recollection of doing much more than pass the time with DeShawn Parker. *Why am I here?*

"Bryce." DeShawn lowers the bat and sticks out a slender arm to shake hands. "My apologies for not introducing myself sooner."

"That's alright. Trust me, you weren't missing anything."

"It did look like you had a bit of a rough start," DeShawn says. He turns and smacks another ball into the outfield.

"You could say that."

"How were you feeling today?"

"How did it look? Pretty terrible."

"No...like, before. When you woke up."

Bryce thinks back to the parking lot. "Not so good. Nervous. Scared to death to be honest."

"I bet. You know that expression, "I'm off my game?" DeShawn asks.

"I feel like it was invented especially for me," Bryce says.

"Well, we all have those days."

"You're DeShawn Parker. I don't think you ever have those days."

"I do," the man laughs. "I do. But it's my job to have fewer of them than anyone else. When people count on you for clutch hitting, you don't get the luxury of being off your game."

He smacks another ball.

"I always felt like it wasn't a choice," Bryce says. "You know, you have good days and bad. Sometimes you're on and sometimes you're off. Lady luck and all that."

DeShawn seems to consider this.

"I think there's truth there. But maybe not as *much* truth as you think. For me, being on my game is more of a choice than the hand of fate."

Bryce is confused. "Are you saying I chose to have a lousy day today?"

"Not consciously," DeShawn says. "But let me ask you this. Why are some players clutch hitters and others aren't? If it was all fate, guys like me wouldn't exist."

Bryce considers this. Clutch hitters like DeShawn were called in during the most critical moments of a game. They went up to bat when the stakes were highest--when a game was on the line, and even a base hit could make the difference between a win and a loss.

Bryce had seen it happen. He'd watched Parker nail a game-changing hit dozens of times. He'd even seen him do it at the World Series facing 50,000 screaming fans, with the fate of the whole season hanging on a single pitch. And he'd done it.

Could what DeShawn be saying be true? Was performing under adversity something you learned? Bryce had never even considered it before.

DeShawn hits another ball, emptying the basket beside him. "Baseball will rattle you, Bryce. Players will rattle you. Fans will rattle you. Even your teammates will rattle you."

You got that right, Bryce thinks.

"But have you ever noticed how some people just don't seem to get rattled? You take two batters in a critical point in a game. That's the same stress, same situation, right? But you'll get a different result from each batter. One chokes and the other hits big."

"I guess that's the difference between a clutch hitter and everyone else on the team."

"Here's the thing no one tells you in baseball, Bryce: we're *all* clutch hitters. We all have to learn to face adversity. Every pitch is a challenge. A battle. For everyone. Every fly ball, every base run, every steal. They're all challenges. It's how you respond that matters. And the magic is that you get to *choose* how to respond."

"I guess I chose poorly today."

DeShawn chuckles. "No argument there."

Bryce thinks back to the disastrous events of the day. "I don't know. It's not like I don't know how to hit the ball. I just couldn't seem to do it today."

DeShawn smacks another ball, but says nothing. The sun continues its descent toward the rim of the stadium wall.

"I guess I just need to do things differently," Bryce says.

"That's where you're wrong," DeShawn says. "If you want to perform under pressure, *you need to do more things the same*."

"The same? How can that be true?"

"How many balls have you hit in your life?"

Bryce considers. "I don't know. It must be thousands. Tens of thousands. I couldn't count them all."

"Exactly. And what do each of those times at the plate have in common?"

Bryce squints as the sun splashes across the rim of the outfield wall. "I...I don't know."

DeShawn grabs another ball from the bucket beside him.

"Then that," DeShawn says as he nails the ball into the outfield, "is exactly your problem."

And then the sun winks out.

CHAPTER 13

THIRD BASE

When Bryce opens his eyes, he's back in Dragon Park at home plate.

A sense of frustration floods through him. What had DeShawn meant? What *did* all those thousands of times at bat mean? What did it matter? This was like a scene in a bad movie where someone dies before they can spit out the location of the buried treasure.

The giant field lights come on flooding the diamond. A voice rings through the empty stadium. "Welcome back, kid!" Bryce looks over to see Spooky standing at third base.

"Don't tell me," Bryce calls out. "I know."

He jogs to first base. *Just get on base*, he thinks. Then on to second. *Choose your pitches*. Yesterday, the idea of running the bases like this had seemed ridiculous. Now, it seems as essential to Bryce as any training exercise. Maybe more.

He slows down as he reaches Spooky.

"You need to do it again, Spooky says. "You weren't finished. You came back too soon."

"I don't think so."

"Tell me, what did you learn from Deshawn."

Bryce thought back to his time with the talented clutch hitter.

"That everyone has the opportunity to be a clutch hitter--we all face stress and hardship. What defines you is the choices you make."

"Right."

"But I don't get it. I mean, it makes some kind of superficial sense but..." Bryce trails off, thinking about his last moments with DeShawn.

"*What do each of those times at the plate have in common?*" Bryce says. "That's what he asked me--what makes each at-bat the same."

"Ahhhh," Spooky says.

"What?"

"Look, kid. You've hit the ball a million times. You should know. What *do* they have in common?"

Bryce thinks. "Well, it's not hitting the ball, that much I can tell you. But...maybe fundamentals? You know--the basics of baseball. How to hold the bat, watch the ball. Stuff like that."

"Mmmm. Close. Fundamentals have their roots in something else.

How do you develop fundamentals?"

"Practice, I guess."

"No guessing about it. You practice and practice and practice. Your coach tweaks along the way, but most of it is just repetition and time on the field."

"But what does that mean for clutch hitting?"

`"Ahhh."

Spooky takes a couple of steps away from Bryce, raises his hand, and rubs his thumb and forefinger together. It's a strange gesture, as if he's suggesting something is expensive.

Immediately the lights in the stadium dim, down, down to almost dark.

How is he doing this? Bryce wonders.

"Okay, kid." Spooky says. "Picture DeShawn Parker coming up to bat. What does he do?"

Now, *this* is something Bryce can understand. He's watched hours of the man hitting--he can call up a mental image as surely as pressing play on a video. Especially now that he's just met him.

Bryce is about to close his eyes and conjure up a memory of DeShawn at bat, when he catches a flicker of movement at first base.

What--

As if from thin air, a figure is materializing next to the base. One minute the base is empty, the next a ghostly image is flickering beside it. Bryce stares in disbelief as the pale figure resolves into a first base- man, in full Python uniform.

As Bryce watches, another figure appears at second base. Then a fuzzy pitcher materializes on the mound. Bryce slowly turns a full circle at third base as more players materialize around him. Outfielders. Base coaches. A shortstop.

As Bryce watches in awe, he hears a low, growing roar like the sound of bees in a distant hive. All around him the stands are beginning to fill with fans, hazy and holographic. He can see the waving pennants, the fan jerseys, the team hats.

This is no ordinary day, sports fans!

For once, Bryce and the voice in his head agree.

Another KACHUNK and the scoreboard lights up.

HOME: five VISITOR: five
INNING: ninth
STRIKE: two OUT: two BALL: zero

A tie game at the bottom of the ninth, Bryce thinks. *And two strikes, no balls.* His stomach tightens. A batter's nightmare and a pitcher's dream.

"What is this?" he asks quietly.

"Eyes on the plate, kid."

Bryce looks to home plate where a ghostly catcher crouches flanked by an umpire.

There's movement to the right. And Bryce sees a shimmering DeShawn Parker, his thin body flickering and translucent, step into the batter's box.

Bryce is transfixed.

The hive-like hum of the ghostly audience fades away. All eyes are on DeShawn. It's so still you can hear the flags ripple along the stadium wall.

The pressure, Bryce thinks. *So much pressure.*

DeShawn raises the bat.

At the mound, the ghostly pitcher cocks his arm and throws. DeShawn swings.

Bryce barely sees the ball. But he hears that sound, that magical sound. That sound that you get just a fraction of a second to enjoy before the roar of the crowd--the second-best sound ever--drowns it out.

Even before the crowd begins to roar, Bryce knows the ball is gone. Then in a flash, it all vanishes. The roar of the crowd, the score-board, the ghostly players--all gone in an instant.

Bryce turns to Spooky. "What was *that*?"

Spooky dismisses the statement with a nonchalant wave. "Parlour tricks, kid," he says. "Tell me what you *saw*."

"I have no idea!" Bryce says.

"Focus on DeShawn. What did you see?"

"I saw a gifted hitter," Bryce says. "The best clutch hitter in history."

"Then look again."

Spooky nods toward home plate again and Bryce turns to see that ghostly DeShawn has reappeared. This time, however, the stadium and field are empty. It's just Bryce, Spooky, and the ethereal image of DeShawn.

DeShawn steps up to bat. Lifts the bat. Swings. Drops the bat. Then he begins to run for first base, but freezes, his flickering form stopped mid-stride on the baseline.

"Well?"

"Well, what?" Bryce says.

"What did you see?"

I don't know what he wants me to say, Bryce thinks.

As if reading his mind, Spooky says, "Again." He rubs his thumb and finger together, and the ghostly DeShawn begins to reverse trotting backward to home plate, where the bat rises up as if by magic into his hand and then through a reverse swing, and onto his shoulder.

Then he lowers the bat and steps, herky-jerky reverse video style, out of the batter's box.

Spooky runs it again. DeShawn steps into the box. Swings. Runs. Then he reverses it.

Then he runs it again. And again.

On the fourth pass, Bryce begins to see things.

"Stop," he says to Spooky. DeShawn freezes mid-swing. "Go back to the beginning."

Spooky nods knowingly.

"It's..." Bryce searches for the right word. "Like...like a poker tell. He does the same thing each time."

The DeShawn "video"--that's the only thing Bryce can think to call it--begins to run in slow motion as Bryce speaks.

"First he touches his hat. Pulls it down just a little. Steps into the box--right foot, left foot. Digs in his cleats. Left once, right twice."

Now that Bryce knows what to look for, it seems so obvious. He's seen DeShawn do this a hundred times before.

"Then he plucks up his pant leg on the right leg. Lifts the bat once." At the plate, DeShawn's image seems to follow Bryce's voice, as if instructed.

"He takes a short swing. Then lifts the bat again. Shrugs his left shoulder."

"You got it, kid."

"I'm not sure I understand exactly what I've got."

"I could show you this guy at bat a hundred times," Spooky says, "and every time it would look the same. Not similar, but *exactly the same.*"

"Okay."

"It's not a poker tell," Spooky says, "although you're not far off. Poker tells are unconscious--you scratch your nose when you have a great hand or clear your throat. You do it without thinking.

It's a ritual, but unconscious. This is similar, but instead of telling his opponent something he's telling *himself* something."

"I don't understand," Bryce says.

"All those little movements," Spooky says. "They're a ritual. And they tell his body and mind, *We're about to do this thing we do.*"

Realization dawns on Bryce. "That's what DeShawn meant by doing more things the same."

"That's right. You need to go back to *ritual.* Everyone has a ritual. A routine, a set of habits that they repeat when they do what they're best at. It comes from the thousands of hours of practice. The first few times you do something, you're all over the place. You're finding your way, figuring it out. But over hours, days, months, years, the things that stick become ritualized."

Bryce thought about his own ritual. *Grab your cap at the back with your right hand. Tug it down. Knock the left cleat with the bat. Adjust your glove.* The list went on.

"But how does that help with adversity? With getting through tough times."

"When times get tough," Spooky says, "The tough return to ritual. They use their habits to put them in a place where they perform at their best. Think of it as a switch to put you on your game instead of off."

Spooky snaps his fingers, and the ghostly DeShawn vanishes. The field lights come back up to full brightness.

"There's a saying," Spooky says, "That amateur's practice until they do it right. But pros practice until they can't do it *wrong.* The difference is ritual. Your ritual is what puts you in that zone where you're more likely to succeed. It turns *off* the stress response and turns on your ability to do what you do well. The ritual is a shortcut. A way of letting you *choose* how to respond to adversity."

"If it's so habitualized," Bryce says, "then why am I doing things so wrong? Have I forgotten my rituals?"

"Close. We always have rituals, kid. Your problem isn't so much that you've forgotten your rituals, but that you've replaced them with new ones. Ones that don't work well when the going gets tough."

Like drinking and sleeping on the couch, sports fans!

Spooky looks at him as if reading his mind. He reaches into his pocket and pulls out the now-familiar battered baseball.

"Don't forget, kid. Rituals aren't just for baseball." He hands Bryce the ball.

The lights go out and Spooky turns and walks into the darkness of the outfield.

Bryce looks down at the ball. In the dim light of the moon, he sees a set of words inscribed in the worn leather:

Remember your rituals.

SPOOKY'S RULES

1. One base at a time.
2. Choose your pitches.
3. Remember your rituals.

CHAPTER 14

BRYCE AND LOUIS

The sun is just peeking over the edge of the enormous parking lot when Bryce arrives at Dragon Park.

He'd opened his eyes early that morning to find the baseball still clutched in his hand. The line *remember your rituals* staring back at him. He'd closed his eyes to try to get back to sleep--the Dragons had the day off--but gave up within minutes.

Now at dawn, he's dressed and ready to hit the field to reacquaint himself with his habits.

Your good habits, says the voice.

Bryce drops his gear in the locker room and walks down the tunnel to the field. Halfway there a familiar sound echoes down the tunnel.

Who else would be here at this time? he wonders. *On an off day?* But even as he thinks it, his stomach drops with the knowledge of exactly who it is.

Bryce peers around the edge of the tunnel mouth catching a surreptitious glimpse of home plate. It's as he thought: Louis stands at the plate, a bucket beside him, effortlessly smashing balls into the distant reaches of the outfield.

Bryce ducks back into the tunnel.

Well, sports fans, the voice says, *it would appear our hero is a little intimidated.*

"Shut up," Bryce mutters.

That's my replacement, he thinks. The new Bryce Holloway hitting balls into the outfield like it's no big deal.

And he turns and slips back down the tunnel, and out of Dragon Park.

CHAPTER 15

THE FOURTH PITCH

Bryce spends the day in a funk.

Baseball was my whole life, he thinks. *What am I supposed to do now?* Even the sight of Stefania's protruding stomach, which would have delighted him just a few weeks ago, now makes him feel only shame.

I'll be unemployed. I'll be a has-been trying to be a father.

What will he tell his kid when they ask about his work? What about bring-your-kid-to-work day? Will he bring his son or daughter to the local bar? At some level, he has to find a way get his life back on track.

The day passes slowly, downward, darkly in an ever-deepening spiral.

By the time dinner is over, Stefania is obviously nothing but thankful when he tells her he's headed out.

By nightfall, he's back at the stadium. This time, the park seems truly empty. Other than the occasional security guard making rounds, the entire place is his.

Skipping the bleachers, Bryce stands in the darkness of the ball diamond waiting. There's no sign of Spooky.

Bryce pulls the tattered baseball from his pocket. He turns it in his hands.

A few moments later, he's swinging the bat like it might be his last chance.

THOK

CHAPTER 16

THE SLIDE

The first thing Bryce feels is his stomach sinking, as if he's falling. The feeling lasts only an instant and then is blown away by a blunt impact that sends a numbing sensation through his left leg and hip.

The strong rays of the sun fly into his face, blinding him momentarily.

He has time to think, *I'm sliding*, and then his foot hits something solid. *A base*, he thinks, *but which--*

--his thoughts are cut short by a deafening roar, so loud he *feels* it as much as hears it.

He knows that sound.

Bryce opens his eyes. A cloud of dust is settling, and through it, Bryce can see the hazy image of an umpire standing over him. The ump's mouth is open, but Bryce can't hear anything over the immense roar of a stadium crowd.

But he doesn't need to hear the ump, because the raised clenched fist says it all: Bryce is out.

Bryce gets to his feet and brushes the loose dirt from his uniform.

You win some, you lose some, he thinks, and waits for the crowd to settle.

But the crowd doesn't settle. If anything, that rumbling, hissing roar grows even louder.

What the hell is going on?

Bryce turns to check the scoreboard and three things register.

The first is that this is Foxchester Field. This was his home before he went to the Dragons--the place where he left behind the awkward and anxious moments of his rookie years. A place where he learned more about baseball than he'd learned in the previous decade. If there's a place outside of Roarke County that Bryce would call home, this is it. Not even the plush penthouse condo he shares with Stefania gives him a feeling of home like this place.

The second thing he notices is that Foxchester Field feels like it's on the brink of *exploding*. The place is packed, yes. There isn't an empty seat anywhere, and even the aisles and exits seem jammed. *There must be fifty thousand people in here*, he thinks. *In a stadium built for forty-five*. But it's not just the numbers. As his eyes scan the stands, it's as if he's surveying a boiling sea of human energy. People are screaming. A rain of clothing, garbage, and beer cups is streaming out onto the field.

Reflexively, his eyes flash up to the scoreboard, in time to see the OUT-number change from two to three.

And that's when he realizes. *These people aren't cheering*, Bryce realizes *They're furious.*

And he knows, with a flash of dismay, exactly where he is.

For a long time, Bryce would claim--with all the bluster and passion of a man who knows he's lying--that it was the third base coach's fault.

"He told me to keep going," Bryce kept telling anyone who'd listen.

And for a time, there were plenty of people who would listen. When your star player--and the captain of the team--ignores the base coach's call, and tries to turn a run-of-the-mill single into a double and an extra run by skidding into home plate like a superhero, people want to know *why*.

Bryce's answer was that the third-base coach *told* him to. Signaled him to keep going.

But that isn't true, sports fans.

Indeed, it wasn't. It was obvious from reviewing the tape--"So obvious any *idiot* could see it," one newspaper would say, with special emphasis--where the coach can be clearly seen telling Bryce to pull up at third.

But Bryce just kept on going. Didn't even hesitate. Stamped a foot on third and just picked up speed. He headed for home like a horse for the stable where, despite the dramatic slide, he was leisurely tagged out by a catcher who, it can also be seen from the replays, can't believe his luck.

And no wonder. That disbelieving catcher had just taken out Bryce Holloway the Foxchester star with ease. And in doing so he'd ousted Foxchester from the World Series.

Which is why right now, as the dust settles at home plate, fifty thousand home fans are screaming in shock and anger at the hubris (or sheer idiocy the newspapers will soon say) of superstar Bryce Holloway.

Bryce himself is in shock when he realizes the moment he's reliving. *This was the worst day of my life*, he thinks.

Maybe second worst, sports fans.

True perhaps, but for the moment, Bryce just wants to get away from the crushing sonic spotlight he's under. So, he lowers his head and walks toward the dugout.

Behind him, the visiting team has exploded into jubilant celebration. Their one-run lead--a lead that Bryce has allowed them to keep-- has clinched them a place in the series. The players are climbing all over each other, leaping into the air high-fiving.

In noticeable contrast, Bryce's team sits in absolute silence. If not for the roar of the crowd, you'd be able to hear a pin drop. His teammates who aren't staring off somewhere else are glaring at him--some in anger, but many in sheer disbelief.

"What were you thinking?" one asks him, then walks off without even waiting for an answer.

Bryce once told a reporter that those moments in the locker room, after his bizarre gaffe cost the team a series run, were perhaps the worst of his career.

Now reliving them again, Bryce is quite certain he was right.

Normally boisterous, the locker room now has all the feel of a brisk, efficient mortuary. Men shower and change in silence, then pack and leave. As the door opens with each departing player, Bryce hears chaos filter in from the hallway outside--reporters asking question after question all related to the same thing: Bryce's screwup.

In what seems like a matter of moments, the locker room is empty.

Bryce stands at his locker staring blankly at the back wall. He knows the reporters will outwait him. But he can't bear to face the questions.

He leans his head forward until his forehead hits the cool metal.

And that's where he stays.

"You can't hide forever, you know."

The voice startles Bryce so badly he thinks he might have actually fallen asleep standing up.

He blinks and turns to see a man he's met before, but never spoken to. Tall, solid, still straight despite his age, he seems to balance the impossible task of appearing imposing and friendly, all at the same time.

The man is Rudolph Sandler, the iconic former captain of the Foxchester Falcons. He is the man who once led this team to the World Series three times.

He is, Bryce thinks, the opposite of Bryce in every possible way. Bryce looks around the locker room. It's just the two them. "Everyone's gone," Rudolph says in his clipped, South African accent. "Just me."

Bryce nods. He's not sure what to say.

"You can't hide from them," Rudolph says again.

"I know," Bryce says. "I just can't face it right now. They're going to want to know why I did it."

Rudolph lowers his large frame to the locker room bench, but says nothing.

"I imagine you want to know why I did it, too," Bryce says.

Rudolph considers this. "I would think it is you who would like to understand why."

Bingo, sports fans.

Bryce, of course, already knows.

I've been through this before. Why am I here again?

"Do you know why you did it?" Rudolph asks.

"The third-base coach told me to keep running!" Bryce blurts the sentence out.

"I see," Rudolph says.

"What?" Bryce asks, defensively.

Rudolph stands up slowly and looks around the locker room. He begins to walk the room, his fingertips trailing the locker bays. "I have many fond memories of this game. This...*calling* that is baseball. Many. Do you know what my greatest memories are?"

"There'd be a few to choose from," Bryce says. "Three World Series wins to start with."

"Yes. Those were...rewarding," he says, choosing the word carefully. "But my greatest memories, many years later, are all from this very room."

Bryce is surprised. Surely his greatest memories are from the field? The fans, the wins? The big hits? Hearing that sweet *sound* so often in front of so many people?

"Yes. Here. For every moment of triumph on the field, Bryce, there are so many other moments here. Moments of despair. Of hope. Of exhaustion. Of sheer joy. It's here that we celebrated together, strategized together, fought together. This is where we learned, lived, and played as *one*."

It's true, Bryce realizes. The moments on the field are adrenaline- fuelled and dopamine-driven, but the time here behind the scenes...it's something different.

"This is where a ballplayer lives his life, Bryce. Here in the locker room with his team."

Bryce feels something well in him, then spill over. Tears come to his eyes. That was why this was so hard. It wasn't just losing a game or a series. It wasn't a bad play. It was the disconnection from his team. It was letting them down. It was the loss of his *friends*.

He hangs his head. *How could I have forgotten this?*

"Don't feel bad, Bryce. We all do this. We forget the important things. Unfortunately, sometimes we lose our grip on what matters most just when we need it the most."

Bryce can't speak. He just stares at the floor.

"Unless you plan to order a lot of pizza," Rudolph says with a chuckle. "I think you will have to leave here at some point."

Bryce reluctantly smiles. It feels good. "You're right about that."

"When you leave, you will have to tell the reporters and the world a story. But more importantly, you will have to tell yourself a story. It can be a story about Bryce, the hero. Or it can be a story," he pauses, and looks around the locker room, "that honors this place. This team. Your team."

Rudolph walks to the door, then pauses. He's staring at the light switch on the wall.

"When I was captain, I always tried to be the last one here. I would know I'd done my job that day if it was *me* who turned off the lights. That meant I'd stayed until the end supporting my team. Even if they didn't need anything, I knew--and they knew--that I was always here for them."

"I wish you all the best, Bryce," he says.

And then he flicks off the lights, leaving Bryce in complete blackness.

CHAPTER 17

HOME PLATE

Bryce opens his eyes to find himself in the Dragons' locker room. *Every locker room is different*, he thinks, *but somehow the same.* "You got that right, kid," Spooky says, startling him.

"Do you have to keep doing that? You scared the hell out of me!"

Spooky's wide grin gets even wider. "Sorry, kid. Sometimes a little jolt is just what the doctor ordered, though. You know what I mean?"

Yeah. I do, Bryce thinks. He scans the room again. "You know, I thought I had this figured out. One lesson per base, four bases. I thought we'd be standing at home plate right now."

"If you think the sport is about home plate, then...to use an old cliché, you've already lost."

"But Coach Teller told me you win the game by getting on base. That you can't win without it."

"Tell me this, kid," Spooky says. "Why'd you ever start playing ball in the first place?"

Bryce opens his mouth to speak. And then...nothing. His mouth just hangs there open like a catcher's mitt.

I don't know the answer to this, he thinks. "Come on, kid."

How could he have come this far, through these many years, and not know the answer? He's been through countless interviews and endless conversations about his career. *Has no one ever asked me?*

The answer was no. And as far as Bryce knew, he'd *always* wanted to play ball. Always *played* ball.

"I wanted to win the World Series," Bryce says, at last. That, at least, is true. He *did* want to win the World Series.

"Why?"

"Because that's what every pro wants."

"Why?"

"Because that means you're the best."

"Why?"

"This is going to get tired pretty fast," Bryce says.

"Seriously, kid. Why does it matter if you're the best?"

Now this, this was a different question. Why did it matter? All his life he'd been driven to a World Series ring. Why?

Spooky continued. "Here's the thing, kid. Victory is a fleeting thing. Being the best--it's satisfying, but it doesn't last. There's always another year, another team, another superstar, another first-round pick. There's always someone who will beat your record, someone who will be better than you."

"Better than me?"

"Yeah. You can't be best forever."

"That seems like you're telling me to not even try."

"What I'm telling you kid, is *that there are other things in life that are worth trying for.*"

Bryce thinks of Stefania. Their unborn child. All the tough times he has put her through when she was expecting, coming home at unknown hours of the night completely disorientated. He knows he has to make it up to her.

"Exactly," Spooky says.

"That's creepy, you know. The 'reading my mind' thing."
"What can I say, kid? I'm a people person."

Bryce looks around the locker room. "I am too. It's just...it feels like you have to do things yourself sometimes."

"That's your ego talking again," Spooky says." We have this tendency to turn to others in good times. That's when our personal story feels best. When our ego isn't threatened by those around us. In fact, when we need others the most--when you need your team--is when trouble comes knocking. When the stakes are high, and the pressure is on, *you need other people in your life.*"

"But only one guy can swing the bat," Bryce protests.

"Congratulations, kid. You just discovered the big lie of baseball."

"The big lie?"

"Yep. The game teaches us to be heroes. The legends of baseball are the home-run kings. The no-hit pitcher. The base stealers. They're positioned as lone heroes, but none of it is possible without the team."

"So what do I do now? What's the lesson here?"

"I don't give lessons, kid. Your job is to remember what you already know. Let's just say my job is to put a little extra spit on the ball."

Bryce hangs his head. Reluctantly, he tries to recall again that awful day. "That night," he says, finally. "After I met Rudolph. I walked out of there determined to do right by my team. To follow Rudolph's example."

"And?"

"And then I lied to everyone. I told them the third base coach signaled me to do it."

Spooky leans back against the locker room wall.

"I betrayed everyone," Bryce says, sadly. "But the weirdest thing was that for a while I believed the story. I began to see the third-base coach *telling me* to keep going. It was like...like I changed what actually happened in my mind."

"Ego's a funny thing, kid. Or not so funny, I suppose." Spooky grins his broad smile.

"Real funny," Bryce says. "That was a horrible time."

"So, what happened?"

Bryce thinks back to the awfulness of the following week. The nightmares. The feeling of being on the outside. Of having lost his team.

"I broke down," he says, at last. "I just broke down. I told the story.

The truth. It was awful. But it was...sort of great somehow."

Bryce thinks back to that moment. He'd understood at the time that he needed to tell the truth. *The truth will set you free*, they say. But now he understands something deeper.

"Things got better after. A lot better. That was when my career truly took off to a new level. But..." He trails off.

"But what?" Spooky prompts him.

"I always used to ask myself why I lied. But now I think that was the wrong question."

Spooky nods. "When you're right, kid, you're right."

"I just want to make sure I understand perfectly. I mean...trust me, I do *not* want to relive that day again. Any of these days, for that matter."

"The important question is this, kid: do you understand why you kept running that day?"

Bryce nods. *That was the question that mattered.* "Yeah. I do. Well--now I do."

"And?"

"I kept running," Bryce says, "because I wanted to be a hero." Spooky just nods and reaches into his pocket.

"Even when you're alone," Spooky says, "You draw on the strength of others in times of adversity. That might be your friends. It could be the thought of your children. It could be God. But the point is this: *adversity is a team sport.*"

And with that, he hands Bryce the baseball. Inscribed next to the worn stitching are five words:

Adversity is a team sport

When Bryce looks up, the locker room is empty.

SPOOKY'S RULES

1. One base at a time.

2. Choose your pitches.

3. Remember your rituals.

4. Adversity is a team sport.

CHAPTER 18

THE GAME

In the pre-dawn darkness, Bryce awakens to a single striking thought: Today is my last day in baseball.

Strangely, the broadcaster in his mind has nothing to add. No admonishments. No judgment.

It's my last day in baseball, Bryce thinks, *and I feel...*

How did he feel? He knows how he *should* feel: awful. Like he was losing a limb. Or two.

Yet all he could feel was a strange sense of tranquility. *I'm about to face the greatest challenge of my life and I feel at peace.*

He looks at the baseball on his bedside table. "Okay, buddy," he says. "Time for one more game."

Dragon Park is packed. It's a sold-out game.

That's in no small part due to the game itself--a victory tonight will make the Dragons league champions and send them to the World Series. A loss and the season is over.

But Bryce knows there's more than just the usual season-ending energy in the air. With Louis, the new "Wonder Kid," now on the roster, even the most casual of baseball fans has put two and two together: Bryce Holloway is done. The result is a stadium jammed with fans, there to see a legend leave the sport and perhaps witness the birth of another.

At a word from the coach, Bryce strides with his team onto the field. He sneaks a quick glance at the second row behind the plate, but there's no sign of Spooky.

He feels a sense of loss. He's only known the strange little man for a few days, but it's as if Spooky has been with him his whole life.

In a way, he has, Bryce thinks. After all, Spooky has just seen him through some of the toughest times of his life--again--and the idea of never seeing him again saddens Bryce, but he takes a deep breath and shakes it off. *One base at a time, right?*

That's right, sports fans! the voice says.

And in that instant, as if reading his mind, the stadium erupts in a roar.

It's game time.

The game begins well. Bryce finds himself on base more than once and is brought home for a run. After five innings, the Dragons lead by two runs and Bryce feels good. Alert. Alive. Aging legs and all.

If we can win this thing, he thinks, *I can go to the World Series. Even if it's the end of my career, I could go out big.*

The thought carries him through another inning and another run. But by the seventh inning, the tide has turned.

By the ninth, that tide is threatening to drown them.

Bryce sits in the dugout nervously checking and rechecking the scoreboard.

It's not like it's going to change without me knowing, he thinks. But he can't help himself.

It's the bottom of ninth. The Dragons are three runs down, their chances of winning the league title slipping away by the moment.

But they're not out.

A critical error by the defense and some great batting by the Dragons has created a situation worthy of a television drama: The Dragons have loaded the bases. A home run right now would put them ahead by one run, and end the game, and the season.

Bryce fidgets, squirming like a kid on a little league bench, as he watches the next Dragon step up to bat. The crowd, too, is restless. Bryce can feel that end-of-game energy, amplified by the stakes and the insanely dramatic, bases-loaded situation that the Dragons have found themselves in.

The batter fouls off the first pitch, but there's power in that swing.

The crowd roars.

Just a little to the right and that would have been over the wall, Bryce thinks.

Indeed, as if he's listening, the batter hammers the next one to right field. Bryce can hear the thunder of the crowd rising as the ball climbs higher....

...And then falls short of the wall. An easy out.

Bryce hears his name over the speakers, echoing through the park. "Next up for the Dragons, Bryce Holloway."

This is Bryce Holloway's chance to show his stuff, his inner broadcaster says. A big hit now and the Dragons would be crazy to send him down.

Bryce feels a glimmer of hope building inside him.

It's true, he thinks. *I could bring the team into the World Series.* Bryce walks to the plate feeling the roar of the crowd. He steps into the batter's box, kicks his cleats into the red earth,
and looks toward the pitcher at the mound.

The first pitch comes in, a curveball, and Bryce swings, nearly spinning himself right out of the box. Reflexively he looks up to the scoreboard, already knowing what he'll see.

STRIKE: one

He takes a deep breath. *One base at a time*, he thinks. The second pitch. He swings again.

STRIKE: two

Choose your pitches, he thinks.

The third pitch comes in wide, just off the corner of the plate, and Bryce lets it go.

BALL: one

The fourth pitch is almost identical, but it isn't to Bryce's liking and he lets it go by.

BALL: two

What am I doing wrong?

He hears a voice in his ear, and he turns.

"What?" he says to the umpire. The ump simply shrugs.

The voice comes again and this time he recognizes the New York accent.

Remember your rituals.

Bryce takes a breath. Kicks in his cleats--right, then left. Pulls the back of his cap down. Adjusts his gloves.

And raises the bat to his shoulder.

Immediately he can feel the difference. Everything slows down. He watches the pitcher wind up, release.

Bryce knows right away it's wide and watches the ball zoom past him. He looks up at the board to confirm what he already knows.

STRIKE: two BALL: three

For a ballplayer, Bryce knows this is the definition of adversity. It's a full count. Two out. Bottom of the ninth. The next pitch could send Bryce back to the dugout and end the game. Or it could send the Dragons to the World Series.

And it's all up to Bryce.

The roar of the crowd begins to build.

Bryce looks to the pitcher who waits patiently at the mound, inscrutable.

He thinks of Spooky.

Of Coach Teller. Sid Mayes. Rudolph Sandler. Of Mel.

Of Stefania.

The din of the crowd is almost deafening.

Faintly, as if from far away, he hears the voice of the umpire, *play ball, kid.*

The last word echoes. *Kid.*

A memory surfaces in Bryce's mind. It is a vision of Spooky calling out to him from second base. *Whoa there, kid. That ain't the way.*

(Was that just two days ago? It seems like a lifetime, he thinks.)

He remembers how strange it was to hear that lone voice in a stadium. He hadn't liked it. It wasn't...*natural.* Ball fields weren't for individuals.

And then it hits him.

Ball fields aren't for individuals. They aren't for heroes. They're for teams!

Adversity, he hears Spooky say, *is a team sport.*

In that moment, it's as if the stadium has gone dead silent. Bryce turns to the umpire and calls a timeout.

An uneasy rumble rolls through the crowd as Bryce walks toward the dugout. Mel meets him halfway there.

"What the hell is going on?" Mel asks.

"Pull me," he tells Mel, in a low voice.

"What are you talking about? You're on fire, Bryce. Just go hit the damn ball!"

"Pull me. Put in Louis," Bryce insists. "Call it an injury, whatever."

"Just do it."

Mel squints at him, as if trying to decipher Bryce's motivation. Then he simply says, "Fine."

"Louis," he yells back to the dugout. "Get in there."

Moments later, the crowd erupts yet again as Louis strides up to the plate. Bryce can only imagine the chaos of the radio and television commentary.

This, sports fans, is unprecedented. Unprecedented.

For a moment, Bryce feels a pang of regret so strong he almost grabs Mel by the shoulders. He wants to scream, "Wait!" Wants to shake Mel and say, "It was a mistake! Put me in! I can do it!"

But he thinks back to the week behind him. To the tattered baseball in his jacket pocket.

To Stefania.

And the feeling passes.

What does not pass is the tension. Bryce may not be at bat, but he's watching Louis with every fiber of his being. The crowd, which was near-riotous the moment before, has hushed to an eerie silence.

Louis steps into the batter's box. Kicks his cleats into the dirt. Lifts the bat to his shoulder.

And waits for the adversity that is every pitch.

Later, Bryce will tell reporters that everything happened so slowly in that moment, that he could actually count the stitches on the ball as it connected with Louis' bat.

It was only partly true.

Bryce was, in fact, counting stitches. But on a different ball. On a yellowed, tattered, barely held together baseball, covered with a few lines of writing, and a lifetime of memories.

And how do you explain that?

It is the last lie he will ever tell a reporter.

CHAPTER 19

FIFTH BASE

After the reporters, the champagne, the kudos, and, what Bryce is sure is the greatest sense of *team* he's ever felt, Bryce finds himself back in the stands alone.

A grand slam in the bottom of the ninth, he thinks. And then he wonders if Louis realizes just how much the rest of his career might pale in comparison to that very moment. Bryce himself can't help but wonder the same thing about his own career. *Was that the high-water mark?*

He knows he did the right thing. But there's that part of him that can't stop wondering *what if? What if it were me that hit that grand slam?*

Could he have? With Spooky's rules? He had no idea and never would.

As the post-adrenaline lull begins to take hold, he wanders down to the field. The lights are out. The scoreboard is a dark monolithic block above the stadium wall. There's no noise save the muted hum of distant traffic.

He stands at home plate, stares at the vast space of Dragon Park, and thinks, *so this is how it ends.* You make it all the way to the edge of the World Series. Then you pull yourself out of the game and get sent down.

This is what it adds up to, he supposes, this life in baseball. You strive, you hope. You win, you lose. And then, it's over. Faster than you ever imagined it could possibly end, it does end. Just like that.

Lost in his thoughts, Bryce barely notices his feet begin to follow a familiar pattern walking the line from home plate to first base. It's a trip he's taken many times.

"One base at a time," he says out loud as he reaches first and, in that moment, he's surprised by a sudden, newer sense of loss. *Spooky's gone*, he thinks. Back to wherever, or whenever, he came from.

What a week it had been. By third base, the pattern of Spooky's lessons had been more than obvious. Every time he returned from a surreal trip to his past, he'd found Spooky there to teach him a new lesson about adversity.

Not teach, he corrects himself. *Remind.*

Now, meandering from first to second, and then to third, the lessons return.

One base at a time. Choose

your pitches. Remember your

rituals. Adversity is a team

sport.

Bryce speaks them aloud as he walks, then pauses at third, staring at the last stretch to home plate. How often had he run this stretch? How often in his mind? In the dusty ballpark of his youth? In the big leagues? Too many to count.

Would this be his last?

Well, sports fans, the broadcaster says, *this has got to be a pivotal moment for Bryce Holloway.*

Bryce shakes his head and chuckles. *If this is how it ends*, he thinks, *I guess I should make it count.*

In his mind, he imagines the sound.

The solid THOK of wood on leather.

The ball leaving the bat, almost faster than the eye can follow. *Now*, he thinks, and he pushes off third base, his body uncoiling like a spring.

And there's the hit. Bryce Holloway is making a bold move for home. This is going to be close, sports fans!

Bryce's legs pump as he accelerates into a full sprint for home. *There's Holloway moving fast. The ball is coming in, it's going to be close!* His lungs are burning. He runs as he's never run before, running for the crowd, and for his team, and for baseball, and for Stefania, and running just for the sheer joy of the game.

His foot stomps down on home plate.

He stops, bends at the waist, his breath heaving. He looks up at the scoreboard.

It stays dark.

In the distance, the traffic hisses. A horn sounds.

"You're out," he says softly.

"Fuggedaboutit," says a voice behind him.

Bryce would recognize the voice anywhere. He turns to see Spooky standing on the baseline between third and home--the very spot Bryce has just run through.

A flush of joy moves through Bryce. "Hey kid," Spooky says with a grin.

"Hey Spooky." Bryce is grinning right back as he walks the baseline back to the midpoint.

"You know," Spooky says. "Once upon a time there were variations on baseball that had a fifth base. It was right here, more or less. Those games are lost to the sands of time, I suppose. But I suspect the lesson of the fifth base has been lost, too."

"The lesson of fifth base?"

"Lemme ask you this, kid. That voice in your head, when did that start?"

Bryce's mouth falls open and he begins to stammer. "What...I..."

"Easy, kid. We all have a voice. The shame isn't in having one, it's in knowing when to listen to it and when to shut its yap."

Bryce takes a deep breath. No one--not Stefania, not his teammates, not his coach--knows about the voice.

"It was quiet for a long time," he says. "It came back louder this year."

"Yeah? What else happened this year?"

Bryce thinks. "The drinking, I guess. Well, it got worse this year anyway." He kicks at the dirt around the batter's box. *I feel like a kid in detention.*

Spooky just waits.

Bryce thinks back. It feels like the voice has always been there. That deep, resonant broadcaster, calling all the plays, critiquing his games, needling him during practice.

"But...it hadn't always been there. It sure wasn't there as a kid. And yes, it had occasionally reared its head, but it had never been so...ever present. So always there. That's why the drinking had started--just to shut the damn thing up. And it had all started to snowball from there."

But what sports fans want to know, the voice interrupts, *is how it started?*

Bryce lifts his head from the red dirt around the baseline and looks at Spooky.

"It was my birthday," he says. "That's when it started." "I guess I was terrified of growing older."

"Ahhhh." Spooky says.

"Ahhh indeed," Bryce says.

"You know why people love baseball?" Spooky says. "Because it's *life*. It's full of curveballs. Full of challenge. Every pitch is adversity. Everyone a threat. An obstacle."

Ain't that the truth, sports fans!

"But here's the thing. *Every pitch is an opportunity.* You see? Our chances to move forward. To succeed. To win. To even be great...they're all in the moments of adversity. Your job is to rise. To accept the pitch." "All your life kid, you've been accepting the pitch. You've been rising to the challenge. Why are you stopping now? Yeah, you're old. Big deal. Your career was always gonna end. So what? The question is, *are you going to rise to the next pitch?* Are you going to just go out or are you going to go out swinging?"

Bryce looks around the darkened stadium. "This was my whole life. Now it's almost over."

"Maybe," Spooky says. "Or maybe it's just another pitch." Spooky turns and takes a long look at the moon rising over the stadium wall.

And with that, he walks toward the darkness of the outfield. Bryce feels his stomach churn.

"Hey!" he calls after him. "What do you mean?"

Spooky turns, and, even in the gloom, Bryce can see his mouth break into a wide grin.

"You don't succeed in spite of obstacles, kid. You succeed because of them."

Then he simply nods once and turns away.

And then the man, his guiding force in the tweed suit, saunters into the darkness.

CHAPTER 20

MEL'S OFFICE

Has it really only been five days?

Bryce stands in Mel Oscar's office. That it's been less than a week since he was last here--less than a week since he received the worst news of his life--is almost impossible to believe. *So much has happened*, he thinks.

So much has changed.

Has it? Bryce isn't sure anything has changed except him.

He gazes about the room, not wanting to sit. Mel would arrive when he arrived and Bryce would accept what was happening. He'd already made peace with that.

His eyes fall on the framed portrait on the wall beside Mel's desk and he steps closer for a look.

It's an old black and white photo, not the original certainly, but it carries the unmistakable weight of history nonetheless. In it are three rows of men in bright white ball uniforms. Those in front sit cross- legged on the turf. The second row on chairs. In the back, a longer line of men stands. Bryce can see Babe Ruth in the center, his round, blunt face showing the barest hint of a smile. At the far left, he recognizes Lou Gehrig, his hands clasped behind his back.

The 1927 Yankees. The greatest team in baseball.

Behind the team, the lowest level of the bleachers is sparsely populated by a few straggling fans and employees.

What the hell?

Bryce leans in closer. Squints.

The photo is old. Grainy. But behind the team in the bleachers, left of the iron girder that extends up to support the upper deck, a man stands in the aisle.

You're kidding me. Bryce leans in for a closer look.

It's blurry and faded, but...the short stature. The suit. The toothy grin. They are unmistakable.

It is, beyond any measure of doubt, Spooky Jones.

Bryce is still staring open-mouthed, at the photo when Mel strides into the office.

"Bryce! Great to see you. Glad you could come in."

This is a Mel that Bryce is unfamiliar with. He's...*cheerful?*

"I know you're busy," Mel continues. "I won't waste your time." He drops a stack of paper on the desk.

"New contract," Mel says. "Three more years. I've got three new sponsors for you, too. They've been hounding me since the game. They say pulling yourself is unprecedented. You've become a baseball legend overnight."

Bryce can't believe what he's hearing. "You're not sending me down?"

"After that game? The fans would skin me alive."

Bryce looks over at the photo. At the blurred image of Spooky Jones in the background.

You don't succeed in spite of adversity. You succeed because of it.

He thinks of Stefania, and their baby, and the words spill out of his mouth before he realizes he's going to say them.

"I'm retiring."

Mel stares at him. Speechless.

"I'm retiring. That was my last game."

"Come on, Bryce. You know what the tough do, right?"

"When the going gets tough? Yeah. They get going. So that's what I'm doing. It's time, Mel."

"You're running away," Mel says, a hint of anger in his voice.

Bryce has considered this, but he knows it's not true. Mel softens. "What are you going to do?"

This, Bryce had not considered. Yet, the answer comes to him and it's as sure, solid, and *right* as that sweet sound of a home run. "There are a lot of guys like me," Bryce says. "Guys who have spent their whole life battling their way to the top." Here, he pauses. "Or at least to what they think is the top."

Bryce looks over at the framed photo of the 1927 Yankees. "I think those guys need to know what to do--"

"--When the going gets tough?" Mel says, the anger gone. "Yeah. When the going gets tough."

"So? What's next, then?"

"I'm going to teach them. Curveball Inc. That'll be the name of my company. I'll coach guys out of slumps. Help guys transition out of pro ball. Teach rookies to manage the insanity of the game. Curveball Inc." He says it again, rolling the name around in his mouth and mind.

Curveball Inc.

It feels good.

Bryce leaves the stadium that day at sunset.

There's no reason to stay--he's learned what he needs to learn. And even if he did hang around the empty bleachers after dark, he has a feeling Spooky has left the building.

He walks across the wide expanse of the stadium parking lot feeling light on his feet. Feeling at peace.

He reaches into his pocket, and pulls out the tattered baseball, yellowed and beaten from years of use.

He looks at the lines of writing along its seams and he smiles. He tosses the ball up in the air and for a moment--just a brief instant--the setting sun catches it giving it a golden glow, like a tiny, spinning sun.

Then it lands in his palm the glow gone.

He slips the ball into his pocket and heads for home. To a beautiful woman. To the mother of his child.

EPILOGUE

The Sound

SIX MONTHS LATER.

Bryce stands, statue-still. His eyes are fixed in the middle distance.

But his ears are listening.

He's listening for the *sound.* That perfect, astonishing sound. The one that when you hear it--which is never as often as you like--changes your whole body from top to bottom. Sends a feeling through you like no other.

He waits.

Patience, he's learned, is indeed a virtue. Life is a game of perseverance of small wins, punctuated occasionally if you're lucky and you persist, by greatness.

Bryce reaches into his pocket and pulls out a tattered baseball. The stitching is coming loose, the leather is almost falling off. In the yellowed leather spaces between the seams, he can see words:

One base at a time. Choose
your pitches. Remember your
rituals. Adversity is a team
sport.

As it always does, his mind returns to a small man in a tweed suit.

And the man's last words, in his strong New York accent:

You succeed not in spite of obstacles, kid, but because of them.

His reverie is broken by the sound.

A rising, musical undulation that is like nothing else on earth. He could listen to it forever.

It's the laugh of a small child. A tiny little giggle, the sound of unbridled joy.

Bryce pauses a little longer just to listen.

The doorbell rings.

"Honey," Stefania calls liltingly. "Can you please get that?"

Bryce opens the door to find a courier on the front porch.

"Mr. Holloway?"

"That's me," Bryce says, and signs for a bulky package.

He closes the door with one foot, and slowly unwraps the parcel.

Inside is an ornate mahogany square box. With gold trim at the edges.

Written on the top is a single word:

KID

Bryce gently opens the lid to reveal a small square of folded paper. Hand printed in beautiful cursive, reminiscent of an eighteenth-century poet, is a single sentence.

You deserve this.

Bryce lifts the paper.

Beneath it is a World Series ring. A thick circle of gold surrounds the face, with a diamond the size of a fist carved into the center. Creating that iconic crest.

Around the perimeter are the words: *New York Yankees, World Series Champions*

Engraved inside is a single date: *1927*

THE END

SPOOKY'S RULES FOR GRIT

1. One base at a time.

When you face adversity, focus on the next smallest step. The size of the challenge facing you may be overwhelming, but there's always a small step that you can handle. Enough of those small steps can get you through anything.

2. Choose your pitches.

When you face adversity, you have the power to choose your response. Adversity is an opportunity to decide how to feel, how to think, and how to act.

3. Remember your rituals.

Everyone has the ability to perform when faced with adversity. Your rituals tell you how to perform well even when you're facing a seemingly insurmountable obstacle--they are a way of turning on your best performance.

4. Adversity is a team sport.

When the stakes are high, and the pressure is on, that's when you need other people in your life. Adversity is a sign to call on help from the people closest to you.

And always remember:

You don't succeed in spite of adversity. You succeed because of it.

Going deeper into the Curveball to face life's obstacles

Colby Sharma would love to take you deeper into his philosophy and keep you inspired to achieve your greatest dreams.

To receive *The Curveball Digital Newsletter* along with superb resources to help you become braver while living your highest potential go to:

www. ColbySharma.com

Stay in touch with Colby here:

www. Facebook: thecurveball426

Instagram: colbysharmaofficial

Linked in: Colby Sharma

Made in the USA
Monee, IL
24 June 2024

60391499R00080